WED TO
KRAMPUS

Cara Wylde was born in Romania and grew up reading fantasy novels. She later transitioned to urban fantasy and paranormal romance, maybe earlier than it was age appropriate. But don't tell her mother! She now writes paranormal romance, science fiction romance and reverse harem.

Arranged Monster Mates is a series she writes with Layla Fae and Eden Ember. These novellas follow different couples, are complete standalone stories, and can be read and enjoyed in any order.

carawylde.com

Wed to Krampus

Arranged Monster Mates

First Digital Edition December 2023

Copyright © Cara Wylde 2023

WED TO KRAMPUS

CARA WYLDE

ALIA TERRA

No one remembers the world before the Shift. It was thousands of years ago, all lost, all forgotten. Scientists and historians say that before, the world was better, brighter, and our planet belonged to us, humans. There were proud countries and bustling cities, and technology was at its highest.

We can hardly imagine all that. There is no proof, no written texts, no pictures of Alia Terra before the Shift. All we know is the face of Alia Terra now. The land haphazardly divided into territories, the walled cities, the poor living on the fringes, barely surviving.

The monsters.

The temples where young virgins can take a DNA test and be matched to one of them. An arranged marriage to a monster is often the only way a woman can save herself or give her family a chance to not starve.

This is Alia Terra. It belongs to the monsters, and we belong to them.

KRAMPUS

They say you're not ready to be in a relationship until you're good on your own. Who says this? Humans. In their books.

I was reading a lot lately. Books about relationships, marriage, loving yourself before you could love another. Self-concept. A lot of self-concept work.

The chapter I was reading as the sun set was about self-concept once more, and I had to put the book down and rub my tired eyes. Maybe it was an obligatory chapter in these modern dating books, but it was the one chapter that never resonated with me. I stood up and went to the bathroom to splash cold water on my face. As the droplets clung to the long hair on my cheeks, I looked in the mirror. How could I work on my self-concept when I knew that the monster I saw in front of me was utterly undesirable? Unlovable.

And why was I reading dating books written by humans when I knew full well that I would never date anyone, human or not?

These days, I avoided going into the town at the foot of the mountain. It was a town where humans lived, and even though they accepted me to some extent, I could see in their eyes that I frightened them. Every time I went into the grocery store or the bookstore, and the tiny humans rushed to get away from me, I felt an ache in my chest. I felt so alone, and sometimes all I wanted was to have someone to talk to. Nothing serious. Just small talk, maybe about the weather, about how this year we were going to have one of the harshest winters in the history of Alia Terra. Talk to someone other than my dog, Frost, and my horse, Snowdrop.

Speaking of Frost, he was snoring in front of the fireplace, lazily spread out on the pelts that covered the floor. And Snowdrop, outside, in the barn, was waiting for me to feed him. Time to get over myself and proceed with the evening routines.

I dried my face with a towel, then walked to the front door and put on my boots and winter coat. Outside, it had stopped snowing, but it had snowed all day, and I would have to clear a path from the house to the barn. The second Frost heard me open the door, he jumped to his feet, gave two barks, as if to say, "Wait for me!", and clumsily ran to join me in the freezing evening air.

Frost was huge, and it had nothing to do with how many times a day I fed him. I'd never seen a dog like him. His fur was dirty white and clumpy in many places, no matter how often I brushed him. I'd found him in the woods when he was a puppy and taken him home. My guess was that someone in town had abandoned him, taken him as far into the woods as they could, hoping he wouldn't find his way back. Their loss, my gain. Frost was a wonderful dog. And a great listener. Seeing how I lived alone, I talked to him a lot.

I grabbed the shovel that I'd left against the side of the house a few hours earlier and cleared a path toward the other soul that lived here with me. Snow-drop was my horse, and he was young and strong. I'd bought him in town many years ago, when my previous horse was too old to pull the sleigh anymore. The man who sold him to me was reluctant. He didn't want to give me Snowdrop, even though I said

I would pay him double. He didn't say it out loud, but I knew what he was thinking. Was I going to eat poor Snowdrop? I assured him that was not my intention, which made him feel embarrassed enough that he eventually sold me the horse.

Doing business with humans when I looked the way I looked was hard. Not that they weren't used to seeing monsters. On Alia Terra, humans and monsters lived in peace, usually in separate communities. They only mingled when they had to. The problem was that they'd never seen a monster like me before, and they never would. Because I'd seen no one like me either. I was the only one of my kind.

Once the path was cleared, I filled a bucket with water and carried it into the barn. The barn was heated, so Snowdrop was as comfortable as possible during the winter. I would've loved to have more animals around, maybe like a proper farm, but it was cold in these mountains. There was snow for most of the year, and the winters were merciless.

"Hello, buddy. You're not lonely, are you?" The horse grunted softly. "No, of course not. That's me. I'm the lonely one."

I shook my head and gave Snowdrop his food, then took a brush and started brushing him slowly. Frost greeted Snowdrop, then paced around for a minute, trying to find a suitable spot to plop himself down. He knew that once we were done in the barn, we were going back to the house, and then it was dinner time for him.

"I'm pathetic, aren't I? And I should just stop." I was talking to both of them, though Frost had closed his eyes and was on his way to dreamland. Snowdrop was eating his hay. "Reading books written by humans. I would read books written by my kind, but are there any? I don't know. I will never know. Love and relationships, and dating, and marriage. What was I thinking buying those books at the bookstore?! You should've seen the look on the cashier's face. I will never date a nice, pretty, kind woman, so why am I lying to myself? There's no one like me, and the humans in town fear me. The women especially, and the children. Last time I went to stock up for the month, a baby in a stroller saw me and started crying. I tried to smile at him, but I only made it worse, and his mother cursed at me and rushed out of the store."

I sighed deeply at the memory.

"I'm a lost cause."

I'd been going to the same stores in town to stock up on food and books, but the townspeople still hadn't gotten used to me.

"I will forever be alone."

At that, Snowdrop turned his head and looked at me with one dark eye. I stopped brushing him and met his gaze.

"Unless... What do you mean by that?" Of course, the horse couldn't speak. It was all in my head. "Unless I go to the Temple. Right. I told you once, and I'll tell you again: I don't want to force a poor woman to marry me."

Snowdrop returned to his hay, and I shook my head and patted him on the back. That was Frost's cue that the brushing was done, and we were ready for dinner.

I said goodnight to Snowdrop and once again reminded him that the Temple was not an option. Back at the house with Frost, I took off my boots and my coat, and followed him into the kitchen. I started preparing dinner for both of us as he watched me with interest from under the kitchen table. He knew to stay out of my way if he wanted his food in a timely manner.

"What do you think, Frost? Should I finish that book? Maybe I can skip the chapter about self-concept." Frost let out a bark to tell me he was listening, but that the choice was mine. At least, that was how I interpreted it. "Do you know what humans say about relationships? That they're only good when two people who love themselves come together. And that you first have to be on your own, be with your own thoughts, and then you can look for someone. I've been on my own since forever. I'm with my own thoughts all day. And most nights, when I can't sleep." Frost let out a growl. "I know, I know. It bothers you when I pace the floor at night." I sighed as I watched the stew cook on the stove. "What do you think about Snowdrop's idea? Because of the agreement between monsters and humans, the Temple should find me a match. If there is such a thing for me. A perfect match. Can you imagine? A woman who is my soul mate. I can't."

Once the food was done, I let it cool. Meanwhile, I poured myself a glass of wine and sat down in an old, creaky chair. Frost emerged from under the table and placed his gigantic head on my knee. I started rubbing him behind the ear.

"But what if I go to the Marriage Temple and speak to the priest? I don't have to let them take my blood for the DNA test. I can have a casual conversation with the priest and ask him what he thinks. I hear the priests who serve at the Marriage Temples all over Alia Terra are wise and have seen plenty. Maybe he knows something about my species. Maybe he's seen others like me. He could give me advice that I can't find in these dating books."

Frost barked once. I got up to pour his food into his bowl. I glanced at the stew that I'd made for myself, but I wasn't hungry. I topped my glass with the last of the wine in the bottle.

"If nothing else, I'll get out of the house a little and talk to someone other than you and Snowdrop. Someone who can say something back." I snorted. "All right. It's decided. Tomorrow, we're going to the Marriage Temple. It's just outside of town, and you can come with me and Snowdrop. Are you excited?"

Frost barked again, and I scratched his head before scooping some stew onto a plate. I felt better already, though it was silly to think the Marriage Temple could help me. At least it was something to look forward to. Most of my days were dull. Tomorrow would be a little different.

AURA

Today it snowed up in the mountains, but the town was spared. This was a good thing, because I really needed to get to the market and sell the scarves and mittens I'd knitted over the past two weeks. With no means of transportation of my own, I had to walk, and walking in the snow was no easy feat. So, I was grateful fate was on my side when I started out in the morning.

The market was in the center of the town, and I lived near the outskirts. I lived in my parents' house, sadly, all by myself. My parents had both passed away the previous winter because of a terrible flu. Many people died last winter, and I sure wasn't looking forward to what was coming this year. My best friend, Mina, told me every day that it was going to be a bad one. She and Joseph were stocking up, especially now that Mina was pregnant with their first baby. Joseph had worked on their house since summer, and most of it was repaired now. Compared to their place, mine was in shambles. With no one to help me, I could only do so much. But I couldn't ask Joseph, since his priority was his wife and their unborn child.

No matter. I was going to be fine on my own. I had a talent for knitting. My mother had taught me, and everyone in town wanted to buy what I made. They needed gloves, socks, scarves, hats, vests, and wool shirts. I made them pretty too, using various colors and models. The patterns had been passed down from mother to daughter in my family, and I was proud to keep the tradition alive. One day, when I had a daughter of my own, I would teach her how to knit.

The money I made was enough to pay the bills, keep the water running, the electricity on... Now that a harsh winter was coming, I was going to have to buy more firewood, but I wasn't worried. If I sold my things at the market twice a month, it was enough for me. And I needed very little to survive.

Spending a day at the market was fun, too. I had friends here, and while the customers browsed, we drank mulled wine and chatted. Everyone was getting ready for Christmas. We knew little about the winter holiday because the books that had survived the Shift were few and incomplete, but we knew it was about decorating everything in pretty colors and lights, and exchanging presents on the first day of Christmas.

The indoors market was decorated beautifully, and after I sold most of my merchandise, I counted my credits and decided I had plenty. I could spend a little to buy a string of Christmas lights to decorate the house. The market closed late in the evening, after sunset. I said goodbye to my friends and started back home, pulling my winter coat tightly around myself. It had snowed a little while I was inside all day, and the snow crunched softly under my boots. I was glad it wasn't snowing now. I just wanted to make it back home, make myself a hot cup of tea and some dinner, and read a book in front of the fireplace until I was too tired to keep my eyes open. Today had been a good day. I could afford to go to bed late and take the day off tomorrow.

I picked up the pace, and soon enough, I was in my neighborhood. As I approached my street, I saw a crowd of people gathered outside, and then I saw flames rising, illuminating the moonless sky. I gasped and ran to the nearest person to ask them what was going on.

"A house caught fire," the old woman informed me.

"Whose house?"

"I don't know, Aura. I can't see anything from here."

I asked a few more people, but we were too far from the fire to see well enough, so no one was sure whose house it was. I pushed my way through the crowd, a knot forming in my chest. It couldn't be... It couldn't possibly be my house.

Someone grabbed my sleeve as I forced my way to the front, and I saw it was Mina, my best friend. She had one hand on her round belly as she clung to the sleeve of my coat with the other.

"I'm so sorry," she said. There were tears in her eyes. "Aura, they're doing everything they can. Joseph is there, helping."

"What do you mean? That is not..." I felt like I couldn't breathe. I gasped for air as I shook my head and pulled my arm free. I ran to the front of the crowd and finally saw it. The fire. "No... It can't be... This can't be happening..." I fell to my knees as I watched the house that I grew up in burn right before my eyes.

A small circle formed around me, and my neighbors pulled me to my feet and tried to console me. Mina hugged me from behind and held me in place when I wanted to run towards my house. There were men who were trying to put out the fire, and it was working, but I could tell it was too late. Now I wanted it to snow.

"Did you leave the fire burning?" one of my neighbors asked me.

"Of course not!"

"A candle?"

"No!"

I didn't even use candles. I'd been living on my own for a year, and I knew how to take care of myself and the house. I almost felt offended that my neighbors would ask me things like that, but I tried to see this from their perspective. One house catching fire put all the other houses in danger. This wasn't just about me. I took a moment to look around me, and I was glad to see that none of the neighboring houses had been affected by the fire. At least there was that. If

I had to suffer, fine. But no one else had to suffer because of me.

Mina hugged me, and I hugged her back. After another hour, the fire was put out, and the onlookers started returning to their homes. My house was in ruins.

"I need to see what I can save," I told Mina.

It was really late, but she nodded. The men who had put out the fire were exhausted and dirty, and as they told me they were sorry and patted me on the back, I could see that their eyes were red from all the smoke, and they were coughing. I felt so bad, but also grateful that everyone had rushed to help. Joseph, Mina's husband, emerged from the ruins covered in soot from head to toe. When he heard what we wanted to do, he didn't go home, though. He stayed with us, and the three of us tried to save as much as we could from the house.

It was getting late, and Mina was tired. Joseph really needed a bath. I had no tears left to cry.

"Come stay with us," Mina said.

"Thank you."

I couldn't say no. I had nowhere else to go, and it was past midnight.

Back at their house, they gave me the room next to the kitchen. It was small, but it was warm and cozy. Mina gave me fresh sheets and towels, then she went to make something to eat for all of us while Joseph took a bath. I didn't know what to do with myself. I just sat on the edge of the bed and stared at the bundle of things we'd managed to save – a framed photo of my parents on the day they got married, a few clothes that were at the back of the closet, an old pair of shoes, and my knitting needles, but now I had no yarn. In the pockets of my coat, I had the money I'd made at the market, and the Christmas lights I'd bought. That was everything.

Mina appeared in the doorway.

"Come on. Wash up a little, then you must eat something."

"Mina..." I looked at her, my eyes swimming in tears. "What do I do? Where do I go?"

"You don't have to go anywhere, silly. You can live with us." She rubbed her belly and smiled. "The baby will be here soon, and I'll need a hand."

I smiled too, knowing full well that I couldn't live with her and Joseph. I had no intention of being a burden to them.

"Come on." Mina took me by the hand and helped me to my feet. "You need food and a good sleep."

"My home is gone."

"Honey, home is where your heart is. And we're here for you. It will be all right, you'll see."

I nodded, but I didn't quite believe her. I followed her into the bathroom and let her help me wash up. I felt like a zombie. I moved on autopilot, and when Mina asked me something, I answered without being aware of what I was saying. Later, in the kitchen, as Mina filled our plates with food, I couldn't even look at her husband. His eyes were still red, and he was coughing in a handkerchief.

"Don't worry," he said. "It'll go away. Aura, you must look on the bright side. You weren't home, or you could've been caught in the fire."

"Or I could've stopped it," I said. My voice sounded weak and tired. "What do you think caused it? I didn't leave the fire burning, and I don't use candles."

Joseph shrugged. "It could've been a short circuit. We'll never know, I guess."

"The house was old," I said. "And after my parents died, I didn't have the means to repair what was broken."

The truth was that we didn't have the means to fix things when they were alive, either. And my father hadn't been a great handyman. With doing repairs, he always delayed it until the last moment. A serious storm and water dripping through the kitchen ceiling had been needed to make him take out his toolbox, tinker aimlessly for two days, then finally hire someone to fix it properly.

Not that I was criticizing him. I missed him with all my heart, and I didn't care that he sometimes procrastinated on fixing things around the house.

The house that was no more...

I could barely eat when I knew I had no place to live. I forced myself, though, because Mina had cooked even though it was way past midnight and she was tired.

"We'll all think more clearly tomorrow," she said, reaching over to squeeze my hand. "You don't have to think about anything right now, Aura. You can stay with us. I told you already." She looked at Joseph.

He nodded. "Yes, absolutely."

Mina and I had been friends since first grade. We met on the first day of school, and since then, we'd been inseparable. I knew she would've done anything for me, because I would've done anything for her.

"Thank you. I love you so much, and I'm so grateful you're my friends. But..."

"But?" Mina furrowed her brows.

"I don't want to be a burden to you if I can help it. There is a way... Another way..."

Mina let go of my hand and straightened her back. She and Joseph exchanged a glance. I knew they would not like what I was about to say.

"The Temple. I can send my blood, and maybe their DNA test will find a match for me."

"No!" They both said it at the same time.

"I won't let you do that," Mina said as she stood up from the table and turned her back to drop her dish into the sink. She furiously scrubbed it.

"I'm with my wife on this one," Joseph said. "An arranged marriage to a... monster? Aura, what you need is a good husband. A human husband. Someone you'll marry because of love."

"Who would take me now that I have nothing?"

They fell silent. No one in town was rich. We all scraped by, and when two people got married, it was partially because they liked each other, and partially because they could build a better life by joining their assets.

"Look, it's something that's worth trying," I said. "I will send a blood sample and see what happens. See if there's a match for me. I don't have to go through with it, okay?"

Mina shook her head and walked out of the kitchen. I could feel that she was so disappointed that she couldn't even look me in the eye anymore. Joseph stood up and started clearing the table. I helped him with the dishes, and we said goodnight.

I knew this was not what my friends wanted for me. An arranged marriage to a complete stranger who wasn't even human. I didn't want it for myself. But what choice did I have?

KRAMPUS

It was a long way to town, so I started early in the morning. I harnessed Snowdrop to the sleigh, and Frost was more than happy to prance in the snow ahead of us. He knew the way. As we approached, he turned around and slowed his pace. He also knew that the people here were never quite happy to see us. Fortunately, the Marriage Temple wasn't in town, as it was an institution of importance that needed plenty of land around it. As far as I knew, all the Temples were self-sustained, and they employed servants who took care of the grounds, the gardens, and the greenhouses. The monsters, as we were all called, and the human females who were their matches needed an intimate space in which to meet and bond their fates.

This suited me well. It meant I would not meet too many people.

I pulled at Snowdrop's reins as we reached the gates of the Temple and one of the young servants – a man with long dark hair, all dressed in white – opened the gates and motioned for me to go in. Two servant girls were waiting, and they took Snowdrop and Frost, assuring me they would both be watered and fed. I was impressed with the way they were treating me. These people who were serving were humans, and none of them were giving me the nasty looks I usually got in town. I guessed they were just used to seeing all kinds of monsters every day.

It turned out that the priest was officiating a ceremony, and I had to wait. They asked me to do so in a room, and I was curious to see who the newlyweds were, but then decided to respect their privacy. I waited patiently, thinking about the questions I had, wondering if he could give me answers. Half an hour passed, and finally, the door opened, and the priest slipped inside and took a seat in the opposite armchair. Between us there was a small table, and on it, there was coffee and pastries. I couldn't eat, so I just drank two cups of coffee, already feeling more awake than I should've probably been. I was almost jittery, or maybe those were just nerves.

"How can I help you, Mr..."

"Krampus."

I swallowed heavily as he cocked an eyebrow, then nodded. I wondered what his reaction meant. He was a middle-aged man with salt and pepper hair, but still strong and athletic for his age. His eyes were deep and blue.

"You can call me Krampus," I added quickly, clearing my throat and straightening my back. "Though I'm not sure if it is my name, or the name of my species. It's what I've called myself always."

"Very well." His features softened. "How can I help you, Krampus?"

"I was wondering if... No, let me start from the beginning. I have been alone for a long time. I live up in the mountains, where I have a cabin and plenty of land. I grow food, I hunt, but I have no one to share this life with. It's been lonely. And I was wondering if the Temple might help me. I'm not sure if I should even try to look for a bride, but..."

"Why do you say that?" he interrupted me.

I spread my arms wide, as if inviting him to take a better look at me. The look in his eyes remained unchanged, as if he didn't understand my point.

"I am covered in fur from head to toe." Dark brown fur, to be more exact. "I am almost ten feet tall, and so wide that I barely fit through your doorways." Browsing the shelves at the local bookstore was a nightmare each and every time. "I have fangs and horns, and when I come into town once a month, people rush to cross the street and get away from me as fast as they can."

The priest nodded. I fell silent and waited for him to say something. He leaned into his armchair and poured himself a cup of coffee. He wanted to fill my cup too, but I refused.

"And you said you don't know if Krampus is your name or what your species is called," he said. "That is interesting to me. How come?"

"After the Shift, I woke up in the middle of a barren field, with no memory. Everything around me was in ruins. For days I wandered, trying to find shelter, or someone who could tell me what had happened. I saw cities that had been burned to the ground, and the bodies... so many bodies..." I shook my head, hating to think about those days. "I was lost for a long time. Every time I met a human, they would run from me. Finally, I came across a community of wolfmen who were rebuilding a town. I stayed with them for a while, helped them, and they told me about the Shift and about how everything that was before was no more, and how it was up to us to rebuild the world. When I asked them if they'd seen any of my people, they said I was the first of my kind they'd ever encountered. All the monsters, aliens, and even humans I spoke with after said the same thing."

"You've been on Alia Terra since before the Shift?" His eyes widened, his coffee forgotten. "How old are you?"

I shook my head. "I don't know. I can't remember anything from before."

"Indeed, it must be so lonely to live like this."

"It is."

"I have seen no one like you either," he said. "I know you live somewhere in the mountains, in isolation, and I've heard about you from the townspeople. It's true that they fear you, but that's only because you're one of a kind. They know about wolfmen, and lionmen, and some of them have even seen dragons. As for me and everyone who serves at the Temple, we've seen so many monsters, of so many shapes and sizes, that we are not afraid. We feel nothing but gratitude for the work we are doing. It is important work to bring together species and facilitate the connection and union between us. Alia Terra is stronger and more prosperous this way."

"That sounds... beautiful."

"It is. That's what I believe. And I also believe that if you're looking for a bride, we can find her for you."

"I need to give you a blood sample..."

"If you wish."

"And you really think there's someone for me out there? Someone who would want me."

"A perfect match is a perfect match. The DNA test is never wrong."

"And it has never happened that a human female refused to marry the monster she was matched to..."

"Not in my time at the Temple, no. And I have heard nothing like this from my predecessors."

I took a deep breath and considered his words. What did I have to lose?

"We can take a blood sample right now. I'll have a servant do it. It's a simple process. Of course, once we find you a match, there is a fee."

"I am happy to pay it. I can pay it right now."

"No need. We first provide the service, and once you are happy with it and you accept the woman that we have found for you, the exchange will be made. These are the rules."

"I understand. The rules sound fair."

"So, shall we do it?"

I nodded firmly. "Yes."

I stood up at the same time as the priest. He left the room, and I didn't know what to do with myself. I started pacing, hyping myself up in my head. It only took five minutes for the priest to return with a young woman servant. He told me he had another ceremony to officiate, and that he hoped to see me soon.

As the Temple servant drew my blood, I noticed I was feeling better. I'd come here not knowing what I would find and what my conversation with the priest would be. I hadn't found out anything about myself, and I wasn't surprised. After all this time, I knew my chances of meeting someone who knew about my species were close to zero. But I found out there was still hope for me. If the priest was certain the test would find me a match, then I owed it to myself to give it a try.

I left the Temple in high spirits. Since I was close to town, I thought of dropping by the bookstore to see if they had anything new, but then changed my mind. Precisely because I was in high spirits, it was better to return home and spend the day dreaming about my future wife. I didn't need the people in town to remind me how hideous I was, and that if the Temple found me a match, she would probably have the same reaction upon seeing me.

Maybe I could prevent that from happening. Maybe there was a way. Things would be so much easier if only she could see my heart before seeing my face.

AURA

The letter came in the mail a few days after I sent my blood sample to the Marriage Temple. Mina gave it to me without a word. I went into my room, sat on the bed, and stared at the letter. I couldn't bring myself to open it, so I didn't. I didn't open it on the first day, but on the second day, I felt a little bit braver. It was a simple note that informed me the Temple had found a match for me, but it said nothing about who I was matched with. I'd hoped for more information. It also said to go to the Temple when I was ready, and that when I arrived, they would send word to my soon-to-be husband.

It sounded like there was no pressure, which was good, because I didn't feel ready. Later, at dinner, I placed the open letter on the table and watched for Mina's and Joseph's reactions. Mina sighed, and Joseph reached for her hand.

"If this is what you want to do, Aura, we understand."

"I don't," Mina said, quickly. "Speak for yourself. I don't understand, and I never will." She fixed me with her gaze. "You have a home here, with us. Why do you have to go and... and... offer yourself to a monster? A literal monster, Aura! Have you ever seen a monster?"

I frowned. "There are many species on Alia Terra... It's true they rarely come to our small town..."

"Except for that beast I saw in the bookstore last year! I've never gone to the bookstore since. Not that I have money for books..."

I sighed. "I went to the bookstore countless times, and I never saw him," I said.

The truth was, I never had money for books either, and I only went to browse the shelves. Then I realized it was only making me sad, and I stopped going. A few times, I did go specifically to try to catch a glimpse of the furry beast the townspeople kept talking about. Apparently, he came down from the mountain once a month, and didn't have a regular schedule or anything like that. Our paths never crossed, so I gave up. Or more like I had other things on my mind. And a monster stalker, I was not.

Plus, I was pretty sure he wasn't as scary as people said he was.

"I heard there are beautiful monsters too," I tried. "Like... phoenixes. And dragons. I mean, dragons are big, but handsome when they turn into men."

Mina's gaze softened. "I hope with all my heart that your perfect match is a beautiful monster."

I fiddled with the letter. "They mentioned nothing about him. About his kind or even his name. I don't know if that's the protocol."

"And you're sure you want to do this."

"Yes. I think I am."

"I support you then. And if you change your mind, our door is always open. You will always have a place in our home. You're family, Aura."

"I know. Thank you."

We ate in silence for a while, then Joseph started telling us about his plans to renovate the kitchen next year and make it bigger. Mina didn't seem excited about the prospect of having her kitchen turned into a construction site for months, but she didn't want to discourage him either. She loved he was doing so much around the house. He also had a plan for expanding the house by building another room.

They had so much work to do, and the baby would come soon... They didn't have any time or space for me. No matter how much they loved me, and I loved them, I wasn't their responsibility. And no, I wasn't ready to marry a complete stranger, but it wasn't like I had any other good options.

I decided to go to the Temple the very next day. Before I could change my mind. Before Mina could change her mind about supporting me in this.

I was lucky that the nearest Marriage Temple was at the edge of our town. It served the neighboring towns, and from what I'd heard, it officiated many arranged marriages. I personally didn't know any women who'd gone to the Temple, but I knew there were plenty. This was not something people talked about openly. When a young woman sent her blood to the Temple, she only told her family and her closest friends, if she had them. And at some point, she simply disappeared. If she had family, they would receive the credits the husband had paid for her, and they would have a better life, at least for a few years. If she had no family, truly no one heard anything about her again.

No one would hear anything about me either. If I went through with this, for a while, my old neighbors would wonder where I'd vanished. Mina and Joseph wouldn't say anything, and then people would forget. Maybe they would miss my scarves and mittens. I could only hope...

I packed lightly, since I hadn't been able to save much from the fire. Mina insisted I took two of her dresses and a pair of boots that were newer than mine. We said our goodbyes, shed our tears, then Joseph helped me into his sleigh and took me to the Temple. There, we hugged, and I almost begged him to take me back when I realized I might not see him and Mina again.

Who knew where my arranged husband lived? There weren't a lot of monster communities in these parts. The mountains were harsh, the woods deep, and the winters a nightmare. I'd heard dragons lived in lush kingdoms. No one in their right mind would choose this climate over a warm, beautiful place in the south. If I was lucky, maybe my husband was from somewhere nice and sunny.

At the Temple, two servant girls took me in. They gave me a room that was comfortable and all mine, with a four-poster bed, a huge fireplace, and even a bookshelf.

"We will send word to your arranged mate that you have arrived. For now, rest. We'll bring you lunch later, and help you bathe and get dressed. He might be here later today, or tomorrow."

"Does he live around these parts?" I asked.

One of the girls smiled as she took my coat and inspected it. "This needs a thorough cleaning. Do you mind?"

"Not at all. Thank you. But can you tell me anything about my... um... mysterious husband?"

"We have been asked to be discreet."

With that, they took their leave. I stood there, baffled, not knowing what to think anymore. Why was his identity such a mystery? Was this normal? But I was here now, so... what else could I do but go along with it?

When the servant girls returned with my lunch, they seemed on edge. As they waited for me to eat, they debated over what dress was the right one for the occasion, and what to do with my hair.

"So... does this mean my husband will be here today?"

"Yes," one of them chuckled. "We thought we'd have more time to get you ready, but alas... Do you prefer to wear your hair down, or can I braid it for you?"

I tucked a wild curl behind my ear. "I'd rather wear it down." My hair was known to have a will of its own. I'd inherited it from my mother. It was long, auburn, and so curly that it was hard to tame.

"Are you finished?" the other servant girl asked me.

I looked at my plate. I'd eaten half of the veggies and barely touched the meat. I felt full, though, or maybe I was just nervous at the thought that in only a couple of hours, I'd be a married woman.

"Yes. Thank you."

"I'll run you a bath then." She disappeared into the bathroom.

Her friend motioned for me to get up from the table and stand in front of her. She held up a few dresses, her brows furrowed in concentration.

"I'm thinking... this one. It goes well with your eyes. What an unnatural color. They're almost golden."

I had my father's eyes. My parents told me that when I was born, my eyes were truly golden. They were so shocked that they immediately changed their mind about my name. Initially, they'd wanted to call me Rosemary, like my grandmother on my mother's side, but when my father saw me, he said the name Aurelia popped into his head. So, they named me Aurelia. Which meant "gold", or "golden", or had something to do with the precious metal. In what language, I had no idea. They called me Aura, for short.

The bath was ready, and the girls helped me wash. I was embarrassed at first, but they were so quick and efficient, and they chattered all the time, and that helped me relax. As they dried me with towels and helped me slip into the dress, I was glad I hadn't eaten too much. It was all happening so fast... Suddenly, my life felt like a train that was going a hundred miles an hour, and I couldn't stop it. The girls brushed my hair and sprayed various products in it, and for the first time, when I looked in the mirror, I realized that my hair wasn't wild. It simply had... character. And it looked the prettiest it had ever looked.

They held up a full-body mirror for me, and I twirled in place. The dress was light blue. The collar and the edge of the sleeves were made of soft, white fur, and the boots the girls gave me were light and elegant, but also warm.

"And this is mine?" I asked as I brushed my hands down the expansive skirt. "I can keep it?"

"You can keep all of it."

"The boots too?"

"Yes."

There was a knock on the door, and my heart jumped in my throat. I swallowed hard and tried to stay calm. It was almost time, but that didn't mean I could lose my head. It was just another Temple servant – a young man. He came in, holding a black box.

"This is for the bride," he said. "Her husband is asking her to wear it."

"Thank you," I said, thinking the box most likely contained a piece of jewelry.

One of the girls took the box from him, but he didn't leave. Not yet. He wanted to make sure that my future husband's wish was fulfilled. The girl opened the box and showed me what was inside.

A mask.

A black mask made of shiny leather. I took it in my hands and inspected it. It was soft to the touch, but there was one problem... There were no holes for the eyes.

"I don't understand," I said, looking at the young man. "How am I supposed to see through this?"

"You're not," he said. His voice was even. He wasn't joking. "Your mate insists that you wear it. May I help you put it on? He is here, waiting for you at the altar. I am to escort you to him."

I looked at the two servant girls, and one of them shrugged, while the other nodded for me to put the mask on.

"Some of them have strange requests," she said. "Strange traditions, I mean."

"Do you think this is a... tradition?"

"If it's a requirement..."

What could I say to that? What was done was done. I was clean, dressed beautifully, my hair was brushed, and my arranged husband was waiting for me. At the altar. They'd all gone through so much trouble to get me ready. I didn't feel ready, but... I knew I would never feel ready. I just had to do it. Get it over with.

I let them put the mask on me, and I immediately clung to the young man's arm. It was odd to not be able to see at all. My world had gone completely black. He guided me out of the room and down the corridor. The temperature changed, which meant we were entering a larger room. I could smell incense. We walked slowly, and I was clinging to him so hard that when he first tried to remove my hands from around his arm, he failed.

"I must leave you now," he whispered to me. "Your arranged mate is here. You will be fine. The test is never wrong."

"Thank you," I whispered back. My voice was shaking so badly that I could barely push the words out.

I let go of the young man's arm. I felt exposed. Vulnerable. I heard him walk away, and a few seconds later, I heard someone else step up to my side. I turned to him, though I couldn't see a single thing. I had the feeling that he was tall, though. Tall and big. Massive.

When he spoke, his voice came from far above my head.

"I know the mask is unexpected, and I'm sorry," he said. "Please bear with me."

His voice was low, and so full and kind. It was the most pleasant, most deeply masculine voice I'd ever heard. I instantly relaxed.

KRAMPUS

Her name was Aurelia, and she was the most beautiful creature I had ever set eyes on. Guided by the Temple servant to the altar, she seemed unsure on her feet, and I could tell the mask bothered her. It bothered me too, to be fair, because it prevented me from seeing her in all her exquisite beauty. The idea had come to me at night, in a dream. What if I could make it so my bride couldn't see my terrifying face until I allowed her to? In my dream, I saw this divine maiden, and half of her face was covered by a black mask. She was walking toward me, her arms held up in front of her, her fingers clinging to me when she finally reached me. She looked up at me, but she couldn't see me, and so... she smiled. Had she been able to see my monstrous features, she wouldn't have smiled, she would've run.

I woke up before dawn and started making the mask with my own hands. Soft leather, sewn beautifully and perfectly, so it wouldn't hurt my bride's delicate skin. And now... she was wearing it. My Aurelia was wearing the mask I'd made for her.

I felt the need to apologize for having her cover her eyes, and I felt her soften at the sound of my voice. That made my heart grow twice as big in my chest. And it was already big... since I was a big guy. Compared to her slight frame, I was built like a mountain. I dared to take her tiny hands in mine. She didn't pull away.

"The mask is... traditional," I said.

Another idea that had come to me as I was waiting for word from the Temple. Since I had no clue where I came from, and there seemed to be no one else like me on Alia Terra, or at least on this continent, I had no culture. No traditions. And I knew humans were big on theirs, so I figured... I might as well invent some for myself. I felt like I needed to explain the necessity of the mask, and it couldn't be that I was ugly and I didn't want my bride to see me.

"Oh, okay," she said in a small voice. "I under-stand."

I squeezed her hands lightly, then I had to let go of her for a minute, so I could pay the Temple for the service it had provided. The priest took his time to count the credits. He put aside the fee that was due to the Temple, then turned to Aurelia.

"What does the bride want us to do with the credits that were paid for her agreement to this arranged marriage?"

She didn't hesitate. "My friend, Mina... Mina Norell, and her husband, Joseph. Can you make sure they receive the money as a gift from me?"

"Of course. It is done. Now, shall we proceed with the bonding ceremony?"

My bride nodded. I took her hands again, and we both listened to the priest's words. I couldn't focus on what he was saying, my mind distracted by the warmth of Aurelia's hands. I was also worried about when the ceremony would be over, because I didn't know what was appropriate... Could I kiss her? Could I take her in my arms and carry her to my sleigh? I'd asked the priest earlier, and he'd told me that different species had different traditions, and it was up to me to choose how to mark our union. I didn't want to frighten my bride, and I also didn't want to give her a chance to touch me too much, because then she would know...

She'd know she'd just married a beast. Though there was nothing I wanted more than to touch her and be touched by her.

I snapped out of my trance when I heard the priest declare us bonded mates. Aurelia turned to me, waiting for me to do something. Or nothing at all. I couldn't know what she was thinking.

"Krampus," she said. Of course, the priest had mentioned my name. "What now?"

I realized I'd been standing there, like an idiot, for at least two minutes, and both the priest and my bride were waiting for me to do something.

"Now... you are mine," I said, though I didn't fully believe it. Not because I didn't believe in the ceremony and the validity of what was happening here, but because I was stunned that this incredible creature was now my wife, and I could take her home with me. "And I am yours." If she wanted me, that was. How long before I had to allow her to remove the mask, and she saw my face and changed her mind about this arranged marriage?

"Yes," she said, simply.

Still at a loss, the only decent idea that came to me was to lift her hands to my lips and kiss them gently.

I lingered, my lips pressed to her warm skin, and I felt something in my stomach that I'd never felt before. Apparently, the priest and all the Temple servants I'd talked to were right – the DNA test was never wrong. I knew, deep down, that Aurelia and I had been made for each other. I'd never known love. Now I did.

"I will take you to your new home."

"I can't wait. I'm sure it is lovely."

Her words made me nervous. What if she didn't like the cabin? What if she didn't like the cold and that we were isolated up in the mountains? What if she'd envisioned a different life for herself?

I kept these thoughts to myself and gently guided her toward the door. The young man who'd brought her to the altar accompanied us to my sleigh and passed me her luggage. I loaded it into the sleigh, then turned to look at Aurelia. As expected, she was standing there, unsure of what to do. I needed to help her up, but before I could do that, I had to cover her hands. She would cling to me, and that could give me away. First, I threw a heavy winter coat onto her shoulders. I'd brought it especially for her, along with a pair of gloves. I slipped the gloves onto her hands, and now it was safe to take her into my arms and gently place her inside the sleigh.

As expected, she yelped and clung to me.

"Please don't drop me," she said.

As if!

"I got you. Don't worry."

Our breaths mingled in the frozen air, and as I held her to my chest, I wanted to lean in and kiss her. I stopped myself. Something told me it was too soon, even if we were bonded and we belonged to each other. I climbed into the sleigh, gently placed her on the fur-covered seat, then covered her with a thick blanket and tucked her in well.

"Are you warm?" I asked.

"More than warm," she giggled. "I'm hot."

If I could blush, I would've. Fortunately, I couldn't, since my face was covered in fur.

"You need to be warm, because where we're going, it's going to be a few degrees colder than here. I... I'm sorry..."

She smiled, but it looked forced. Or frozen. "Don't worry about it. I'm used to the cold. I grew up in this town."

I paused with my hands on the reins. Snowdrop neighed, his breath thick in the air. He was eager to get back home, in his barn, where it was warm and dry.

If Aurelia grew up in this town, then there was a good chance she'd seen me before. Was she one of those people who avoided me when they saw me in the street loading my sleigh with groceries and books that would, sadly, only last me a month, maybe a month and a half, if I was frugal?

No, I couldn't think this way. If I was lucky, she'd never seen me before. But what if she'd heard about me? People talked...

"Are you okay, Krampus?" she asked from the back. "Are we... going?"

"Yes."

Snowdrop needed little encouragement. He was eager, more eager than me, at this point. What did he care? Once we got home, he would eat and sleep, and play with Frost. I'd barely convinced the dog to stay behind. I could tell Snowdrop missed Frost, and Frost was probably howling alone in the house.

What an easy life. To only be concerned with food, shelter, and sleep, and not give a single thought to love.

Up the mountain, on the narrow, snow-covered roads, I made Snowdrop go slowly. Not because I feared we might slip into the abyss below – the horse knew these roads so well that he could navigate them blindfolded – but because I needed time to think. Time to worry about everything that could go wrong once Aurelia and I found ourselves alone in my cabin. And time to calm my racing thoughts and convince myself I could make this marriage work.

Hopefully, all the dating and relationship books I'd read would come in handy at last.

AURA

K rampus.

I hoped he hadn't noticed my reaction when the priest first said his name – a quick intake of air, the stiffening of my shoulders. I tried to control it as much as I could, but throughout the ceremony, my thoughts ran in circles, trying to pinpoint where I'd heard the name before. It felt like a memory. An old memory from my childhood. Something my mother used to say when I was particularly naughty... It had been so long ago, and I didn't want to think of my mother as the sleigh moved through the snow, taking me to my new home.

I didn't want to think of my parents and what they would say now if they saw me. What would I tell them? "I'm sorry, but I see no other way out of this mess." Yes, something along those lines.

I couldn't see anything through the mask, so I had to rely on my other senses. The sharp wind on my cheeks as we advanced to a higher altitude. The sounds the horse made as he trudged through the snow. I felt warm and comfortable. The only part of my body that didn't feel great was my nose. I pulled the blanket up and tucked my chin and my nose underneath. It smelled surprisingly nice, of cinnamon and... vanilla? Come to think of it, everything Krampus had given me smelled nice and felt soft to the touch – the coat, my gloves, the blanket.

I wasn't thrilled by the idea that we were going to a place that was colder than the town I'd lived in all my life. I wondered how far from it his home was. I wondered how many people lived there. Did his kind have a town of their own? A community? How big? How small? Did Krampus have a family? Maybe a sister or a brother? So many questions...

Would I fit in?

This tradition with the leather mask was strange, to say the least. I'd never heard of anything like it. But to be honest, I didn't know much about monsters and their traditions. Hopefully, I wouldn't have to wear it for long. Maybe just for the first day, and then I could remove it and finally see him. See the man I'd married.

I was happy about one thing, though. Mina and Joseph would soon receive a generous amount of money. Knowing Mina, she was probably going to save it for the baby, so he or she could later attend a good school. Maybe a school in the nearest city. The money was my way of thanking them for everything they'd done for me. Since I was married now, sup-posedly to my perfect match, I didn't need it. My husband would take care of me. And I still had my knitting. Maybe this new place I was going to would appreciate my skill just as much as the people in town. And if not, I was still going to knit because I loved it.

Krampus. Krampus.

Where had I heard the name before? As we ad-vanced, the temperature plummeted, and I realized I wasn't feeling hot under the blanket anymore. Just warm.

I was sure it would come to me... The mystery behind my mate's name.

I loved his voice, though. Low and soothing... He talked like he wanted to envelop me with his words and keep me safe. Had it not been for his voice, I would've been a little more scared right now. I was still scared, but it was a level of fear that I could deal with. It was mostly fear of the unknown, not of him. When he'd lifted me into the sleigh, he'd been gentle despite his massive frame. With the gloves on, I couldn't make out a lot. I touched his chest and shoulders, and the feel of them confirmed he was huge. It was all I knew about him.

I couldn't wait to take this mask off. Maybe he wouldn't insist on my wearing it the whole day. I hoped I could take it off once we arrived.

Okay. Krampus. I needed to think harder. An hour had probably passed since we started from the Temple, and I was getting bored. My fingers were itching for my knitting needles. There were two problems, though: one, my fingers would freeze instantly if I took off my gloves, and two, I wasn't sure I could knit with my eyes covered. On second thought, maybe I could. I was that good. So, with nothing to occupy my hands and my mind with, the only thing I could do was... think.

Think hard. Where had I heard that name before?

Finally, my memory yielded and brought to the forefront an image of five-year-old me. I might've been younger. Four? The exact age wasn't important. It was my father's birthday, and my mother had baked a cake, decorated it and everything. We didn't have cake often. Only three times a year, for each of our birthdays. So, it made sense that I was beside myself with joy and excitement. But I was supposed to wait. Dad was still at work, even though it was late, and the cake was waiting on the kitchen counter, so tempting that I could die. My mother kept an eye on me, then told me she was going to wash up, and made me promise I wouldn't touch the cake. We would all have a slice later, when my father came home. Of course, I promised. Of course, I had my fingers crossed behind my back.

The second the bathroom door closed behind her, I was in the kitchen, pushing a chair to the counter. I was too short to reach the cake, but if I climbed on the chair, the cake was all mine. I only wanted a taste. Just a tiny bite. First, I dug my finger into the frosting and licked it. It tasted so good that I couldn't help myself, and I dug my whole fist into one side of the cake, taking a rather sizeable chunk out of it.

My mother caught me elbow-deep in the cake. My face was smeared with frosting, and so was the front of my shirt. She shrieked, which made me jump off the chair and fall on my face. I started crying like it was the end of the world, and she started crying too, and that was how my father found us.

Thinking back, it all sounded funny now. A story I couldn't wait to tell my children. I was glad I'd remembered it. But why had my brain dug it out? Oh, right.

Krampus.

That night, after my mother washed me and put me to bed, she told me I was grounded. First, I wasn't allowed to have cake. She and my father were going to eat it all, and not leave me a crumb. Of course, that was a false threat, because the very next day, I had cake for breakfast. Second, I would get nothing for Christmas. No presents for me. Just coal. And if I complained about it, Krampus would come get me.

Krampus!

She told me he was upset already because I'd destroyed Dad's cake, and he'd come knocking on our door earlier, but she sent him away, promising that I was going to be a good girl from then on. But if I wasn't a good girl, she said she wouldn't be able to save me from Krampus next time, and he would come get me.

"And do you know what he does to naughty children?" she said in an ominous voice. "He eats them!"

I shrieked and hid under the duvet. She laughed and tickled me, and that made me forget about all her silly threats. Because that was what they were. Silly.

I had all the cake I wanted, and I got a pretty doll with long blonde hair for Christmas. And Krampus never came to get me.

Until today.

Krampus

Frost was scratching at the door from the inside when we arrived. Normally, I would've let him outside, but I was afraid he might follow me and Snowdrop into town. He was big enough to break down the door if he wanted to, but he was a polite dog and knew his place. Most of the time.

"We're here," I said as I hopped out of the sleigh and started untucking my bride from under the blanket and her heavy winter coat. "I will help you."

She chuckled. "I hope so. I can't do a thing with this mask on."

Her voice sounded odd. Like she was... reluctant. She was smiling at me, but I wasn't sure if that was her genuine smile. I wondered what had happened. At the Temple, she'd seemed more comfortable – as comfortable as one could be in the given circumstances – but now, it was as if she was regretting her choice.

It could've just been my imagination. I was nervous because we were home at last, and I wanted her to like the place.

"I wouldn't want you to hurt yourself," I said as I took her in my strong arms.

She clung to me at first, but then her body tensed, and she tucked her gloved hands in the large sleeves of her coat as I carried her to the door of the cabin. The snow crunched loudly under my boots. Frost started whining pathetically from inside.

"What is that?" she asked, her head whipping left and right. "What's that sound? Is that a wild animal?"

I could feel her shaking, and my instinct was to press her closer to my chest. When her cheek met with my fur coat, she jerked away. It was a small gesture, but impossible to miss. She hadn't behaved this way when I took her in my arms at the Temple, and now I was really starting to worry. What had happened on the way to the cabin? We hadn't talked at all because of the wind and the snow. Was she upset because of that? Did she think that I'd intentionally ignored her?

"That's Frost. He's my dog."

"Oh."

"You have nothing to fear. He's big, but he's just a puppy at heart."

"Okay."

I opened the door and entered the cabin. Frost took a few steps back and barked excitedly. His tail was wagging so hard that it was in danger of detaching from his butt and flying across the living room.

"Can you put me down, please?" Aurelia asked.

I didn't want to put her down. I didn't want to let go of her. Her weight was insignificant in my arms, but the warmth of her body was everything. It was as if it gave me life. I felt like a whole different person – er... beast? monster? Krampus? – when I held her like this. It was as if my arms had been made specifically for the task of carrying her.

"I'm sorry," I mumbled. "Of course."

"Thanks."

I set her down on her feet, and the first thing she did was to remove her gloves. I wanted to stop her, but I knew it was silly. I helped her take off her coat, then I took mine off, and I was working on unlacing my boots when I saw her reach for the mask on her face.

"No!" My hand wrapped around her thin, frail wrist – so thin, it was like a baby twig in spring – before I realized what I was doing. "You can't remove it."

"Why not?"

"You... can't. It's... tradition..."

She frowned. "And how long do I have to keep it on? What does this... tradition of yours say?"

I opened my mouth to answer, but I didn't know what to say to her. I let go of her wrist when I realized she was squirming. I didn't want to hurt her, and I felt bad when I saw her wince and rub her wrist. I quickly calculated in my head how long it might take her to come to know me. Know the real me, my soul, my heart. I tried to calculate how long it would take me to make her fall in love with who I was underneath my terrifying appearance.

It couldn't be too long. A week? Was a week an acceptable length of time to ask someone to keep their eyes covered around you? She wouldn't be able to do anything by herself. I could let her take off the mask when she was in the bathroom and when she was alone. Would she go for it?

"A week," I said, for lack of a better idea. One day would've made sense probably, even for an invented tradition that made no sense. Three days would've worked too. From the books I'd read, I knew humans considered three a magical number. Seven worked too. Also a magical number. "Only for a week."

"A week?!" Her voice was high-pitched now, and it clearly indicated she was not happy. "But that's so long! Too long! How will I be able to do... anything?"

"You can take the mask off when you're alone," I blurted. I was already regretting all my stupid ideas about stupid traditions. "I will be away from time to time to feed Snowdrop and work around the cabin."

"Who's Snowdrop?"

"My horse."

She thought for a moment. "And how will I be able to meet the others? Like... properly meet them?"

"The others?"

Frost stopped wagging his tail. He'd been looking at Aurelia curiously, waiting for the right time to jump on her and demand rubs, but now he turned to stare at me. I shot him a glance and shook my head.

"Yes. The others! Your family. Your community."

I swallowed heavily. "There are no others."

"What do you mean?"

I could actually see how the color drained from her face. Her cheeks, rosy from the cold, turned pale.

"There's just... me. And Snowdrop, and Frost. And now you."

Her jaw dropped. Her hands started shaking at her sides, and to stop them, she wrapped her arms around herself and tucked her hands underneath her armpits.

"There are rabbits," I offered. "They come around here sometimes." I stopped myself from adding that when they do, I usually hunt them and turn them into delicious stew. I had a hunch she wouldn't appreciate that piece of information. "And deer," I continued. "There's also a crow who took a liking to Frost. They hang out sometimes, and the bird always brings Frost some shiny thing he stole from town."

"So, it's just us. Alone. In a cabin in the mountains." Her voice was low and shaky.

"Yes, I..."

"You don't have... anyone? Family... friends..."

The corners of my mouth turned downward. "You could say Snowdrop and Frost are my family. And that crow."

"The crow…" Was the tremble in her voice a sign of fear or… anger?

"And you. You are my bride. My wife."

I saw her hands fly to her face, and I was ready to stop her from removing the mask, but she wasn't going for the mask. She simply pressed her hands to her already covered eyes, as if she was about to cry and wanted to stop the tears. It was… odd to watch. Now her eyes were double covered.

"I don't know if I can do this," she whispered.

My heart crumbled in my chest. It broke into a thousand pieces, and I went as far as to press my hand to my chest, trying to hold the pieces together.

"We're a perfect match," I said, carefully. "The test…"

"… is never wrong," she finished my sentence. She straightened her back and ran her hands down her sides, then slightly pulled at the skirt of her dress. She was straightening everything, as if she were getting ready to do… something hard. "All right. Okay. I can try."

My shoulders relaxed. A heavy weight was removed from my chest, and my heart felt whole again. This could still work. It was going to work, because I was ready to do anything for my Aurelia.

Well... except let her remove her mask for a week.

"Are... are you hungry?" I knew it was quite the jump from a serious conversation to... food, but I wanted to do something nice for her. I wanted to start taking care of her already, so she would forget about my... oddities.

"I would like to wash up first."

"I will take you to the bathroom."

I gently placed my hand on the small of her back and started guiding her into the living room, then into the bathroom that was on the ground floor. Frost sniffed at her long dress, and I shook my head at him to let him know he needed to give her time. I knew all he wanted was to tackle her to the floor and give her one of his big hugs, but if he did that, I was afraid my Aurelia would tear the mask off and bolt out of the house, never to be seen again.

As we passed the stairs, my stomach fluttered at the thought that I would have to help her up and down for a while. I hoped she'd let me carry her after I fed her a rich, healthy dinner and showed her how much

I wanted to pamper her. She was upset now, I could tell.

"You said I can take the mask off when I'm alone," she said.

"Yes."

I guided her inside the bathroom, and she rested her hands on the edge of the sink. She was standing right in front of the mirror, but she couldn't see herself. From behind her, I looked at us. I was huge, and she was tiny. My face was covered in brown fur, and my horns almost touched the ceiling. If she were to remove her mask right now, she would probably faint from shock and terror. That saddened me. I knew it was true, and no one could convince me otherwise.

What had I been thinking? Going to the Temple, giving them my blood, letting them find me a bride...

If Aurelia did agree to keep the mask on for a week, then that was all the time I would have with her. One week.

The mirror told me she was going to leave me the moment she saw my face.

Aura

He locked me in.

I took a breath, then with trembling hands, took the mask off and looked in the mirror. I couldn't believe this was happening to me. I was married to a monster who was making me keep my eyes covered in his presence for a week! And I was pretty sure this had nothing to do with tradition. He had no family, no community, so how could he have... traditions? I wasn't going to say anything, lest I made things worse for myself, but at this point, I was convinced Krampus was lying to me about something.

One glance around me, and I was stunned. The bathroom was enormous. It wasn't just the tall ceiling, but also the massive bathtub, so big that it could fit, maybe, three or four people, the large sink, the mirror that covered half the wall. The door was huge, as if made to fit... well, him. It was made to fit him.

Even though I hadn't seen him yet, my intuition told me he was tall and wide. When he took me in his arms, I could tell my weight was nothing for him. His hands were so large that one of them was enough to support my back. It made sense that everything in his home would be made for him. I wondered if he'd built this cabin himself. He must've, since he'd said he was all alone here. With the deer and rabbits, and some crow.

In other circumstances, I would've found that funny. The way he talked about his horse and his dog, and his dog's crow friend. I would've been like... "awww... he loves animals". Too bad he was making me wear the leather mask for a week. I couldn't be like "awww" anything, no matter how cute, and lovely, and gentle he was.

Because I could tell he was gentle. The dog, Frost, had sounded excited to have him back home, and I always trusted dogs to be good judges of character.

I turned on the faucet and heard a humming sound coming from the wall. The water turned warm, almost hot, and I had to combine it with cold water. Apparently, living this high in the mountains wasn't the equivalent of an uncomfortable life with no amenities. I washed my hands and my face. That meant the minimal makeup the Temple girls had applied for my wedding ceremony went bye-bye, but it didn't matter since half of my face had to be covered, anyway.

I took my time to pull myself together and make myself look presentable. I brushed my fingers through my long, auburn hair, taming the frizz caused by the typical winter humidity. I adjusted and readjusted my dress, and noticed I hadn't taken my boots off. I did so now, feeling bad that I'd probably made a mess on my way here. It was a good thing there was thick snow outside and that the snow was clean.

When I felt ready, I tried the door, forgetting that Krampus had locked me in. I heard him from the other side.

"Are you wearing your mask?" he asked.

Oh. Right. That was the condition for him to let me out of the bathroom. I quickly put it on and tied the leather straps at the back of my head.

"Yes."

"Do you promise?"

I sighed. "Yes. I have the mask on. I can't see a thing." And it was true. My world was black again.

The key turned in the lock and the door opened. I felt so vulnerable standing there like that, waiting for him to put his hand on my lower back to guide me. I felt like a child. I swallowed heavily and kept my thoughts to myself. This might've been my husband, but really, I didn't know who I was dealing with. I didn't know if the stories I'd heard from my mother had any grain of truth in them. If they did, there was a fair chance it was very little. Still, it was better to be careful and keep my guard up.

He walked me into what I assumed was the kitchen and sat me down at a table. I heard him move around the space, grabbing pots and pans, plates, and whatever else he needed. Soon enough, it started to smell like wine, apple, and cinnamon. He was making mulled wine.

I heard Frost walk into the kitchen. He barked twice, and Krampus said, "You'll have dinner when Aurelia and I have dinner, so be patient."

Aurelia. My parents used to call me that. It sounded strange coming from Krampus, so I had to correct him.

"Please call me Aura," I said.

"Oh. I'm sorry. I didn't know."

I smiled. "It's no big deal. It's just that everyone calls me Aura, and I got used to it."

"Of course."

A cup of mulled wine materialized in front of me, and Krampus went as far as to gently take my hands and place them around it. It burned a little, but I didn't complain. I enjoyed my beverage as he started cooking, adding the smell of roasted potatoes and roast meat to the mixture of cinnamon, nutmeg, and all the Christmas spices I could imagine. I had to admit he knew how to make his home smell amazing. And no one had cooked for me in a year! My mother used to cook before she got sick, and I missed her cooking. Mina had cooked while I'd stayed with her and Joseph, but I'd always made sure to help. When I said that no one had cooked for me, what I meant was... from scratch. As in, they did everything, and I just sat there, waiting for my delicious meal. It was nice.

I felt Frost nudge my leg, and I tentatively reached out my hand to touch him. My fingers came in contact with his wet nose way sooner than I'd expected,

and when I patted his head, I realized Frost was...
big. A big dog for a big man. He let out a sigh of
satisfaction and proceeded to lie at my feet, his paws
right over my toes. I didn't mind it, since he was
keeping me warm.

"Dinner is ready," Krampus said at some point. All
this time, he'd hummed to himself, and I didn't want
to interrupt him. "I hope you like it."

I was kind of starving, and it smelled amazing.

"How will I eat?" I asked as he set the table. I
could hear plates and cutlery clinking, but being in
complete darkness, all I could do was move my hands
uselessly, patting the table here and there, ending up
with my fingers coated in a sauce that proved to be
exquisite.

He laughed and wiped my hands with a napkin
after I'd licked them.

"I will help you," he said, sitting down next to me.
That was when Frost whined and Krampus shot back
to his feet. "I almost forgot about you," he said to
the dog. "Where's my head at? Okay, here is your
dinner." He sat back down again. "Where were we?"

"You said that you would help me..."

"Ah, yes."

And the next thing I knew, there was a morsel of food poking at my lips, and Krampus saying, "Open up."

I blushed to the tips of my ears. I opened my mouth, and he pushed the food onto my tongue. It was a piece of potato with a piece of meat, and they literally melted before I could even chew them properly. I wanted more, even if that meant I had to... open up.

"What about you?" I said through bites.

"I can eat after."

"Oh, no. That's not right. You should eat now. We should be eating together."

"All right. One bite for you, one for me."

We did this for a while, and I almost forgot the situation I was in. I almost forgot that I was having dinner with Krampus, the Krampus from my mother's tales, and that the reason he was feeding me wasn't because it was a sweet and silly thing to do, but because my eyes were covered by a leather mask and I was forbidden from seeing his face.

"Is there any water?" I asked.

He took my right hand and placed it on a glass that had been on the table all along.

"There's wine too. Not mulled," he offered.

"I think I've had enough alcohol for one day," I said.

"A few more bites left," he said.

"I'm full, thank you."

He hesitated. Then, "Can I have them?"

I laughed. "Well, you cooked the whole meal. I think you can have whatever you like."

I blushed again when I realized the implications of what I'd just said. He didn't seem to notice, because I heard him finish his food and mine.

"There's desert."

"I really don't think I can..."

"It's strawberry-flavored ice cream."

"What?" He got my attention, alright. "Where did you find strawberries in winter?"

"These are wild strawberries. I harvest them in summer and freeze them."

"Oh, that makes sense. It must be easy to freeze things here."

"It's winter almost all year round," he said. "So, would you like some ice cream?"

"Yes, please. But only a little. I feel like I'm about to explode."

He laughed thunderously. "Better get used to it, Aura. You need to put some meat on those bones, so I intend to feed you generously three times a day. At least."

I laughed too, but then I heard him go outside, probably through a back door, and silence fell for a minute, and the silence allowed me a moment to think.

"Do you know what Krampus does to naughty children?" I heard my mother say. "He eats them!"

Oh, no. What if the reason he was feeding me so well was that... No. No, no, no. That made no sense. Those were just old wives' tales. They weren't true. It was what mothers and grandmothers told their little ones to make them behave.

As if sensing my distress, Frost came to nudge my leg and spread his massive body on top of my feet. If I flexed my toes upwards, I could feel the shape of one rib. His warmth was soothing. I wished I could see him and play with him properly.

If Krampus hadn't eaten his dog or his horse, he wasn't going to...

Good heavens, I couldn't think like that! This was ridiculous! He wasn't a monster! Except he was...

But, like, not that kind of monster. On Alia Terra, there were no monsters that ate virgins. At least, not that I knew of.

I heard Krampus come back in, and I shooed my dark thoughts away. This was a lovely dinner I was having with my husband, chosen for me by the Marriage Temple, through a DNA test that was never wrong. Everything was fine. More than fine. Everything was as it should've been.

"Careful, it's cold," he said as he fed me one spoonful of ice cream.

Much too brave, I swallowed it whole and got instant brain freeze. Krampus laughed, but he had the decency to pass me a fresh cup of mulled wine to soothe my pain. I had to eat the rest of the dessert like this: one spoonful of ice cream, one sip of mulled wine. By the time dinner was over, I was pleasantly tipsy.

"Now what?" I asked, as Krampus started clearing the table.

He hesitated before answering me. "Are you tired?"

"Very."

After the hearty meal I'd had, all I could think of was sleep. But I was a married woman now.

"Oh. There's a... tradition for the first night of marriage. It can wait until tomorrow."

"No, it's okay. If it's tradition, then we must respect it. Like with the mask."

I was truly hoping my words would make him backtrack and admit there were no traditions involved in anything he was telling me. He didn't.

"All right," he said. "I will be gentle."

KRAMPUS

There was no ritual, no tradition. All the traditions in my life were invented, and because they had no root in the past, I guessed the proper term for them was, in fact, routine. And a lot of them were inspired by the traditions I'd observed in the humans' town. For instance, Christmas was all about decorating the cabin on the inside and the outside. I also decorated the barn because Snowdrop deserved pretty lights, too. I'd read about Christmas in a book that was missing entire chapters. It was called A Christmas Carol, and unfortunately, only the beginning and the end had survived the Shift.

I'd learned that humans had traditions for everything that made up their lives. For when a baby was born, and when someone aged another year. For when two people got married and started a family. I had no experience with any of that. Living all by myself, I'd never seen babies being born, and I'd never lost anyone to... death. Another concept that I didn't quite get. Because I must've been old, so old, yet I felt young, both in my body and my soul, and like death was not something that was meant for my kind. If it ever came for me – the Grim Reaper, as humans called death sometimes – I would've been genuinely surprised.

As I led Aura into the living room and sat her down in front of the fire, I cursed myself for having told her there was a ritual for the wedding night. Because now I was at a loss. I'd read plenty of books to know what usually happened between a bride and a groom on their first night together – assuming it was their first – but did I have the courage to go there? She was mine now, and an arranged marriage between a human female and a monster differed from the union between two humans. It was more definitive, less of a guess. It was, literally, science.

"So, what is it?" she asked.

I busied myself with putting more wood on the fire. Frost emerged from wherever he'd been hiding and went to stand by the front door.

"One minute," I said. "I need to let Frost out."

"In this freezing weather?" she shuddered to make her point.

I laughed. "He'll be fine. He'll explore for a bit, then go bother Snowdrop in the barn."

I went to scratch Frost behind his floppy ears and let him out, then I was alone with Aura. I sat next to her on the large couch, and she turned to me, though she couldn't see me.

"Well?"

I had to come up with something quick. And make it sound real. It had to be something that would bring us closer in an intimate way, but that wouldn't make her feel uncomfortable, or like it was too much, too soon.

"Tradition says that on the wedding night, the male has to... um... inspect every inch of the female's body." I studied her face, but of course, because of the mask, I couldn't read her reaction. "We don't have to do it if you don't want to. And I know it's very cold and... I don't want you to be cold."

"Can we do it with me keeping my dress on?" she asked.

"Yes. I was thinking the same, actually."

"Okay." She nodded as she rubbed her palms on her thighs. "Okay. Can I use the bathroom first?"

I took her hand to help her off the couch and around it, so she wouldn't bump into it, or the coffee table, or the two armchairs and the other pieces of furniture in the living room. Once she slipped into the bathroom, I hesitated with the key in hand. Earlier, I'd locked her in, just to make sure that she wouldn't come out without the mask on. I'd felt bad about it, so I didn't want to lock her in again. I decided to trust her. By now, she knew how important it was to me that she had her eyes covered at all times when we were in the same room, even though she didn't know why.

I waited patiently, thinking about how unreal it was that in just a few minutes, she would allow me t o... touch her. I just wanted to be close to her. I wasn't going to do anything she didn't want, and my plan was to just... brush my fingers through her hair, down her face, down her neck... I fully intended to stop if she gave any sign that she was feeling uncomfortable.

What I wanted was connection. I'd been alone for so long, with no one to hold, and no one to hold me in return, that I craved physical contact.

Aura knocked on the bathroom door.

"I'm ready. My eyes are covered."

I smiled to myself, feeling good for having chosen to trust her. I opened the door for her and took her hand to guide her back to the living room. Her hand shook slightly in mine, and I gave her what I hoped was a reassuring squeeze.

Once in front of the fire, I made her sit on the floor instead of the couch. The floor was covered in a thick carpet and a soft pelt on top of it. It was almost as good as a bed.

"You can lie down," I said.

"Oh, okay."

There she was, spread out before me, and I didn't even care she was covered from head to toe, her face and her hands the only exposed skin. The light blue dress she was wearing had a high neck, and underneath it, her legs were wrapped in thick tights. I knelt next to her and hovered my hands over her stomach. Her chest rose and fell with every breath, and now that she could feel me so close to her, she was breathing faster. I didn't know what to do, where to start.

"One question," she said. "Does it also work the other way around? I mean... does the female have to inspect the male's body after?"

"No," I said quickly. Maybe too quickly. "No."

"Okay."

The last thing I wanted was for her small, dainty hands to touch my face and run over my neck and my chest, only to discover I was covered in miles of thick fur. It was a painful situation, because on the one hand, that was exactly what I craved. Her touch. Her hands on my body. But knowing it would only lead to disaster, I had to bury that desire deep down and be happy with less. Whatever happened tonight, it would be enough.

"I'm ready," she said.

I still hadn't gathered up the courage to touch her, and she was growing impatient. She'd told me she was tired, so if I was going to do something, I had to do it now, before she fell asleep right there, in front of the fireplace. Not that I would've minded it. It would only mean I could carry her to our bed, upstairs, and feel her body pressed against mine.

My thoughts were going in circles. I had to halt them.

I hovered my hands over her face, then let my fingers glide into her auburn locks. Compared to the fur on my body, her long, wavy hair was soft and shiny. It was a pleasure to touch it. I combed my fingers through it a few times until I noticed she was starting to relax. Then I touched her forehead, just above the leather mask. Her skin was warm and smooth. My fingers ran down her cheek and behind her tiny ear.

"That tickles," she said, smiling.

"Sorry."

"It's all right."

"If any of this feels bad, tell me, and I'll stop."

"So far, so good," she chuckled. "It's like getting a massage."

That instantly put a bright smile on my face. Because Aura had just given me the best idea.

Aura

I felt his fingers trace the shape of my shoulders. His touch was feather-like at first, then grew more intense without losing its gentleness. I thought he would move on and run his hands down my chest, but instead, he began to... massage my shoulders.

Because I'd made a joke about how this felt like I was getting a message. And then he immediately started doing just that. It only confirmed this wasn't a tradition at all. He'd lied to me again. Why?

I was about to get angry at the idea that Krampus couldn't be honest with me for one damn minute, but then his fingers dug into a particularly tense spot, and I turned to putty. He was so good at it! He took his time, making sure the muscles were completely relaxed before he moved on. He touched my arms, and that made me feel even more relaxed because it meant he didn't want to do... things to me. Not so soon, anyway. Not before I... asked him?

I wondered if that was what he was waiting for. On the one hand, he kept putting us in situations where we had to be close and intimate – like when he'd fed me earlier – but on the other hand, it didn't feel like he was forcing me to do anything, and he never went too far.

He massaged one arm, down to my palm, then the other. I was about to fall asleep when he moved to my legs, completely ignoring my torso. In his hands, my calves were like jelly. Instead of going above my knee, he descended to my feet, where he proceeded to perform literal magic on my tired soles.

"If this really is your wedding night ritual," I said, "Then us humans should adopt it. Everyone should adopt it!"

He chuckled and continued to massage my feet.

"I'm glad you're enjoying it," he said.

"I'm enjoying it a lot."

At some point, I started feeling hot. The fire burned steadily in the fireplace, and the room had become stuffy. That, coupled with the fact that Krampus was touching me, massaging my body into shameless submission, resulted in beads of sweat on my forehead and my back. The corset of the dress felt too tight, and all I could think of was loosening it a bit. The tights that covered my legs felt uncomfortable. I'd been in these clothes all day long, and maybe they were a little too fitted for my liking. They didn't let my skin breathe.

"Are you all right? Do you want me to stop?"

He must've noticed me squirming.

"No, I'm fine. Don't stop. This is nice. It's just... I'm feeling hot." I bit my lower lip, wondering if I should say what I wanted to say. "Do you think you could... remove my tights?"

I heard him take a sharp breath. He hesitated for a moment, but then I felt his big hands slip under my skirt. He paused at my knees, and I figured he needed some encouragement. I lifted the skirt myself to expose my hips, and finally, I felt his fingers hook into the band of my tights.

"Is this okay?" he asked.

"Yes," I breathed out.

"Are you sure?"

He started pulling the tights down, rolling them slowly over my hips and legs. I thought I would feel cooler, but I was feeling hotter instead. His fingers brushed the sensitive skin of my calves, and I felt myself blush, grateful the leather mask obscured the flush on my cheeks. The tights were off, and when he took my right foot in his hands, I shuddered despite myself.

"You're cold now," he said.

"N-no." I swallowed heavily. "I'm still hot. Very hot. Do you think you could... undo my corset? It's been bothering me for hours."

"Anything you wish, Aura."

Anything I wished... What did I wish?

This was okay, though. This was fine. It was good! Because we were married. It was true we'd only been married for a few hours, but what we were doing was totally normal. And expected.

I sat up so he could undo the laces on my corset, and once I felt it loose enough to breathe more easily, I lay back down. I felt a little better. The dress was still heavy and too warm, but I didn't know if I wanted him to remove it. Maybe a little...

"What else do you need?" he asked.

His face was close to mine. I could smell the mulled wine we'd shared on his breath. His voice was low and husky, and it sent an unexpected shiver through my body. My core throbbed with need, and I felt my panties grow wet.

This was embarrassing. I'd never done anything like it before, had never been touched like this. My parents had taught me that boys were a waste of time, and I'd dutifully stayed away from them. I had other things to do, anyway, and the boys in town weren't that interesting. And now here I was, a silly, inexperienced girl, facing needs I'd never thought I'd have for the first time in my life. The one I was with wasn't a boy either. He wasn't even human. He was a monster whose face I had yet to see. A monster whom I had yet to meet properly.

"I... I don't know," I said. "My legs are tense... right here." I lifted my skirt again and placed my hands on my thighs. Way above my knees. "Do you think you could..."

He went to work with his big, firm hands. His palms were warm, and I could feel something like hair or fur brush against my skin. By now, I knew he must've been one of those monsters who were covered in fur. I didn't know if only parts of his body were covered, or if he was covered completely. It made sense, since he lived up here, in the snowy mountains, where it was always so cold. He must've adapted.

"You can go higher," I said.

He moved his hands up, but when his fingers brushed my panties, he immediately pulled away.

"It's okay," I breathed out. My heart was hammering in my chest. "I'm your wife now."

"You are."

"So, you can... Um... You can do... you know..."

I hoped he knew, because I didn't. I wasn't sure what I wanted, just that I wanted something to happen. I needed him to touch me like he meant it.

"Don't forget you can tell me to stop," he said.

I nodded, and finally – finally! – he touched me between my legs. His fingers brushed my pussy lightly, but the panties were in the way, and I didn't know if he was going to remove them or not, so I decided to take matters into my own hands, and I lifted my hips and pulled them down myself. I only rolled them to my knees, and from there, he removed them all the way. I opened my legs for him, and once again, I was grateful for the damn mask. I felt so aroused and embarrassed at the same time that it would've been impossible to do this if I had to look him in the eye.

"You're so beautiful," he whispered.

I felt his breath on... my thighs. He was so close to me, and looking at me, at my pussy... Oh, I was never going to take the mask off!

"May I..."

"Yes, touch me," I said quickly. "Do something. Anything."

I felt pressure in my chest and in my lower belly. My core was practically screaming for him, and I didn't even care that this whole thing was insane. I was giving myself to a total stranger. Granted, we were married... But it was an arranged marriage, and just yesterday I had no idea what my future would look like. Now I knew. It looked like this: me, lying on the floor of an isolated cabin, begging a monster I'd first heard of in an old wives' tale to touch me.

He cupped my pussy first, and just held his palm there, then slowly parted my folds with two fingers. He was taking his time, which was driving me crazy with lust, but I wasn't going to complain, because I had a feeling it would only make the reward better.

"You're a virgin," he said.

"Yes."

It was one of the conditions imposed by the Temple. Only maidens could send their blood for testing.

"I don't want to take that from you yet."

I wasn't sure what that meant. Sex came in... different shapes and forms, right? He was probably referring to the act of penetration, which was a shame, because I really wanted to feel something inside me right about now. One of his big, thick fingers would do.

"Then what do you suggest?" I asked.

He answered me by brushing the tip of his finger over my clit. I let out a small moan and flexed my legs at the knee, spreading them even more for him. I dug my hands into the folds of my skirt because I needed to hold on to something, and also because I wanted to keep it rolled around my hips, so he could see what he was doing.

He brushed my clit again, then started stroking it gently, just with the tip of his finger. My pussy gushed, and with another finger, he teased my entrance, but didn't push in. I was almost tempted to drive my hips down and force him in, but I focused on my breathing and told myself that taking things slowly was a good idea. If we weren't careful, this could overwhelm both of us.

A few minutes of that, and I was a squirming, moaning mess. A few times, I was so close that I was sure I would explode, but he never let me go over the edge. Not yet. He had more in store for me. When I was just about to complain that I couldn't take his teasing any longer, I felt his breath right on my pussy lips. His tongue darted out and licked my juices from my entrance to my clit, where he pressed his tongue flat until I couldn't take it anymore, and I placed my hands on his head.

We froze.

I froze because instead of finding hair and nothing more, I found horns.

He froze because... he probably wanted to keep them a secret?

"Aura," he breathed against my pussy.

I waited for him to say more. When he didn't, I wrapped my hands around the long, thick horns and pushed his head down.

"Please," I whispered. "No more teasing."

I felt him relax. He didn't tell me to let go of his horns, said nothing along the lines that I wasn't supposed to know he had them. As if they were taboo... They weren't! Plenty of monsters on Alia Terra had horns. From what I'd heard, at least. That was the last thing that would ever bother me about my husband.

He listened to my plea. His tongue started moving in circles around my clit.

"There," I breathed out. "Almost..."

It was easier to pull at his horns and guide him to where I needed him, to the spot that felt like I was going to melt into the floor, than to use my words. He let out a groan when I pulled particularly hard, but didn't complain. He started licking me faster and harder, and I threw all shame out the window and moaned loudly, knowing there was no one who could hear me.

My core was on fire, my pussy walls throbbed with the need to feel something more, and I was sure my juices were all over his face. He licked me until I let out a moan so loud that it was almost a scream, and my body tensed as I came. I felt hot liquid pour out of me, and I had no idea what it was, but he kept his mouth there, on my pussy, and drank all of it. He kept licking me and cleaning me, waiting for me to recover.

I was literal putty in his hands. I couldn't move. My body relaxed like never before, and I let go of his horns. I combed my fingers through my hair, pulling it away from my face and my neck, feeling like it was still too hot and I was too sweaty.

"You're the most beautiful, delicious creature I've ever seen," he said, emerging from between my legs.

My hands flew toward him. I couldn't grab him because I couldn't see a damn thing.

"Come here," I said. "Where are you?"

He laughed, then asked somewhat timidly, "Why?"

"I want to touch you. I want to..."

"No."

"Why not?"

He hesitated, then said, "It's late and you're tired."

I pouted, but I couldn't argue with that. Well, in fact, I could, but I didn't think this was the right time. He was lying to me about something. He didn't want me to touch him, and I could bet whatever his secret was, he was trying to keep it from me by making me wear the mask. I already knew he was a monster, that he was huge, his body was covered in fur, and he had horns. It was all too obvious, so why not let me see him already?

Oh, and I knew he was the Krampus from the scary tales I'd heard in my childhood.

"If you are naughty, Krampus will eat you."

I started laughing, which probably confused him.

Well, that part of the story had turned out to be true.

KRAMPUS

I gathered her in my arms and took her upstairs, into the main bedroom. She was almost asleep, and I felt bad when I had to nudge her awake, so she could change into the nightdress that I'd prepared for her. I was ready to turn my back and walk out of the room when she clung to me.

"No, please stay and help me. I'm so exhausted, I can't even stand."

I'd seen so much of her already. Tasted her. And she was mine. My wife. It was an honor to help her undress and slip into something more comfortable and appropriate. I'd made a mental note earlier that she didn't like corsets, so my new purpose now was to make sure all her clothes were snug, and pleasant, and corset-less. I could knit, sew, and work with leather and fur, and I was more than decent at making clothes, since I'd had to make mine all my life.

When she was ready, I tucked her in and started removing my own clothes. My thick leather belt was the first to go. Then I saw Aura reach for her mask and panicked. I dropped the belt on the nightstand on her side of the bed and rushed to stop her.

"No."

"Please? Turn off the lights, and I won't be able to see anything, anyway."

"I said no."

She sighed, then resigned herself and tucked her hands under the duvet. I waited a beat to make sure she would not attempt to remove the mask again, then quickly undressed, switched off the light, and climbed into bed next to her. I was used to sleeping naked, and it hadn't even crossed my mind that I might need something to cover myself once my bride was here, in my bedroom, in my bed. I was just going to... keep my distance during the night.

She had her back turned to me. I had perfect vision in the dark, so I stared at her back for a long time, until sleep claimed me. I'd never shared a bed with anyone before. Frost didn't count. I would've loved to wrap her tiny body in my arms and pull her in, hold her against my chest and keep her warm, but I couldn't do it. I just couldn't. She'd discovered my horns already. We hadn't talked about it, but when she first wrapped her hands around them, I noticed her shock. She hadn't expected me to have horns. Which made sense. That was another thing, aside from a ridiculous amount of body hair – or body fur – that humans didn't have, so I couldn't imagine a human female wanting her husband to have long, thick, curled horns atop his head. I couldn't let her discover what the rest of me felt like, so I would not pull her into my arms.

I didn't know how long I'd been asleep when I felt my Aura stir. I thought nothing of it. Within seconds, I was back in the land of dreams, but then I felt something warm on my chest. A hand that was exploring. My eyes shot open, and there she was, inches from my face. Her mask was still on.

"Aura?"

She mumbled something unintelligible, which made me believe she was half asleep and unaware of what she was doing. But then she said, "Why don't you want me to touch you?" And even though she stumbled over the words, she sounded like she was waking up.

I couldn't let this happen. Her hands moved down my torso, and adrenaline rushed through my body, waking me up completely. I had to push her away from me before my cock became fully erect, or she was going to feel it. Earlier, when I'd eaten her pussy, I didn't doubt that she wanted my cock inside her. That was because she had no idea what she was in for... My cock wasn't... How could I put this? It was nothing like what human males had between their legs. I'd studied an anatomy book years ago, curious to see the difference between the two species, and that was the first time I asked myself if what I had down there was... normal. Maybe it was normal for me, but not for them, and it was going to take a while for me to be ready to see Aura's reaction when she discovered my horns weren't the only weird thing about my body.

I grabbed her by the shoulders and swiftly turned her back around. She yelped, then giggled, then tried to fight me.

"Oh, come on, Krampus," she said. "We're married." She sounded more and more awake. "We can't sleep in the same bed and not touch. It doesn't make sense." It didn't look like she was going to give up.

What could I do? What could I do?

In the dark, I spotted the belt I'd left on her night-stand when I'd undressed. I reached over and grabbed it, then I held Aura in place and looped the belt around the bedframe first, then around her wrists.

"Ow! What are you doing?"

"What I must," I growled in her ear.

"No, wait."

It was too late. Her hands were safely secured to the bed frame, and she couldn't turn to face me, no matter how hard she tried.

"Seriously? You're going to leave me like this for the rest of the night?"

"I'm sorry."

"No, you're not!" She pulled at the belt, but it was no use. The leather was sturdy. "Krampus! You tied me to the bed! This isn't normal!"

Her words saddened me. She was right. It wasn't normal. Nothing about me was normal. Not the way I looked, not the place where I lived, not my life, my body, the things that I did...

She struggled for a few more minutes, then let out a frustrated sigh and said, "Fine." She hated me. I was sure of it. Now that I'd tied her to the bed, I regretted it and thought of releasing her.

I wanted to undo it. All of it. The scene played out in my head: I would remove the belt, remove the mask that covered her eyes, turn on the lights, and let her see me just the way I was, no clothes, just me. And then... And then she would scream and run out of the bedroom, rush down the stairs, and if she didn't fall and break anything in the process, run outside, in the snow, barefoot and only in her nightdress, and freeze to death within minutes.

Was this scenario exaggerated? Maybe. But I didn't think it was far from what would actually happen, and I didn't want to risk it.

Tomorrow.

I would let her remove the mask tomorrow, and tonight, I would simply enjoy her presence. Even if she was tied up and we didn't touch, the fact that I was sharing a bed with a female for the first time in my life was something to be cherished.

Tomorrow, I was going to be honest with her. No more lies, no more hiding. I was going to let her look at me and judge me for my sins.

AURA

It was impossible to fall asleep with my hands tied to the bedframe. The position was uncomfortable, and on top of that, my left brow started itching because of the mask. Then my nose started itching because of the brow, and all I could do was rub my face on the pillow. I squirmed and fussed, hoping Krampus would notice and decide to untie me.

This was ridiculous!

To make matters worse, I soon heard him snore softly behind me. Of course. He could sleep in peace now that he knew I could barely move a few inches. If I wanted to, I could kick him with my foot, but what good would that do?

I didn't get him. He'd done the things he'd done to me just an hour or two ago, and it had felt amazing, yet he refused to let me touch him. Didn't he want me to return the favor, so to speak? If it didn't matter to him, at least he should've wanted to hold me. We were mates. We were supposed to cuddle!

I was his wife, and it was my right.

I felt him turn onto his back, and within a minute, his snoring became louder. Had my eyes not been covered by the mask, I would've rolled them hard. So, I was going to spend my first night with my husband tied to the bed, unable to see, move, make myself comfortable, or sleep. Great.

I was torn, really. Because on the one hand, he was so sweet and caring. He'd cooked for me, fed me, taken care of all my needs so far. He seemed to have everything ready for me, including the night-dress I was wearing, which had clearly been made for a human woman. I wondered if he'd bought it in town. I imagined him going into the department store, straight to the women's aisle. Now that I knew he was big, with horns and a lot of hair on his body, I was fairly certain he was the monster the townspeople kept talking about. Too bad I'd never gotten a chance to see him. I should've gone out of the house more often.

Okay, so he was so sweet, but then he had these moments when he went all growly and stern, and told me "no". "Don't remove your mask, Aura." Or, "Don't touch me." Or, "We can't cuddle." Well, he hadn't exactly said it in those words, but that was how I translated his actions in my head. It was a pretty poor attitude, and not very sexy, and I didn't know if it was because of me, or because of him.

What was he hiding? I really wanted to see his face. Had he not tied my hands, I would've removed my mask just a little and peeked. He was asleep, and he would've never known. Now I regretted trying to make him cuddle! From now on, strategy first.

No matter how hard I tried to fall asleep, it just wasn't going to happen. I spent hours going in circles in my mind, imagining scenarios, trying to figure out why Krampus didn't want me to see his face. I imagined what he'd say if I simply asked him. I thought about what my week would look like if he didn't let me remove the mask and stuck with the silly idea that it was tradition. I wondered if he was going to tie my hands to the bed every night.

Could I live like this? Could I survive like this for a week? Being spoon-fed and walked around the house? The fact that he did everything wasn't that bad, but I wanted to do some things too. For one, I missed knitting. Which reminded me I had no yarn, since all of it had burned in the fire. Tomorrow, I'd ask Krampus if he could get me some. If it came to it, I was sure I could knit with my eyes covered. No way was I going to spend an entire week completely idle.

I thought about this place. I'd only seen the bathroom, but it was enough to tell me that the cabin was huge. I wondered if Krampus had built it himself to fit him. It had all the amenities, and it seemed to be very cozy and comfortable. It smelled of wine and spices, and delicious food. All surfaces seemed to be covered in blankets and pelts. I wanted to see it with my own eyes so badly.

The bed seemed to be huge, too. Because I knew Krampus was massive, yet as we lay next to each other, we weren't touching. To prove my theory, I extended a leg toward him and felt around with my foot. I couldn't reach him, which meant he was probably sleeping at the very edge of the bed. I briefly considered stretching my body diagonally and trying again. I was sure that if I did that, I would eventually find him, and with an expert shove, I could kick him out of the bed.

I was so tired that my thoughts were becoming sillier and sillier. I yawned and tried really hard to fall asleep. Who knew what was waiting for me tomorrow? I needed rest, or else I wouldn't be able to think clearly.

What if tomorrow I begged him to let me remove the mask? What if I started crying and begged so hard that it would be impossible for him to refuse me? It could be an idea... A strategy.

What if I just... took it off, no matter the consequences? What could he do? Kick me out of the house? Tell me he didn't want me anymore because I broke one of his sacred traditions? Hm. That could actually happen. And then I'd have to return to town with my tail between my legs, and ask Mina to take me in.

The thought that I might fail at this... at being a wife, at making this marriage work was... unpleasant. Krampus and I were meant to be together. We'd been made for each other. At least that was what the DNA test said. I had to trust it, and I had to trust this process, even if I didn't understand it. Maybe he had a good reason for which he didn't want me to see him or touch him. Maybe patience was the answer.

I fell asleep feeling a little calmer after deciding to just... go along with it.

KRAMPUS

I t wasn't usual for me to sleep in, but I did. Even so, I woke up before my Aura. She was lying on her right side, with her back to me, and her arms slightly raised toward the headboard. I felt an invisible claw grip my heart. I'd done that to her. Tied her up so she couldn't reach for me or remove her mask. The mask seemed to help, though, since the sun was high in the sky, its bright rays filtering through the curtains and illuminating the room, and she was sleeping soundly.

I got out of the bed, put on a pair of pants, then moved around to her side. I was careful and silent, not wanting to disturb her. Last night, I'd promised myself that I'd let her remove the mask today. But as I looked at her, then out the window at the beautiful day unfolding before us, I thought... what if I waited one more day? The risk of her seeing me and changing her mind was too big. Especially with our marriage not having been consummated yet, she could easily say she wanted out.

Today was going to be sunny. It was probably one of the last nice, warm days we were going to have this year. I wanted to spend it with her. I wanted to show her around the cabin, tell her about my life here, maybe convince her it wasn't so bad that we were isolated and alone, without a community. We had the mountain all to ourselves.

Well, show her... Not exactly show her, since she wouldn't be able to see anything.

What a conundrum. But there was one decision I could make right now.

I leaned in and started untying the belt from around Aura's delicate wrists. I did so gently, and she only stirred a little. She must've been truly exhausted, or maybe she fell asleep late last night. I rubbed her wrists, which were slightly red. I felt guilty, and I almost couldn't wrap my head around the fact that I'd done this. I'd never planned for it, but last night, when I felt her close to me, wanting to explore my body with her tiny hands, I panicked.

She let out a sigh and mumbled something, then tucked her hands underneath the duvet. I fluffed up her pillow, and she smiled sleepily.

"Thank you."

"I'll let you sleep in," I said.

"Mmm."

She said nothing else and didn't reach for the mask. I put my belt on and went to the closet to find a clean shirt. Before I walked out of the bedroom, I turned and said to her,

"I'll bring you breakfast."

"Mmm."

My heart melted when she murmured like that. It was unbelievably cute.

"I'll knock on the door before I come in."

I didn't say why, but she knew why. So she'd have time to make sure she was wearing the mask. I figured that by the time I made breakfast for the both of us, she'd wake up and get dressed.

"Okay." She yawned.

I slipped out of the bedroom and made my way downstairs.

First things first. I let Frost in and fed him.

"Don't go upstairs," I told him. "Aura is sleeping."

He barked once, and I shushed him. At least he understood. Next order of business – Snowdrop. I put on my coat and boots and went to feed and water the horse. The rule was that Frost and Snowdrop always ate before me in the morning. Frost had lunch and dinner with me, and I made sure to feed Snowdrop before we settled down to eat in the kitchen. The exception was in summer, when it was warm enough for picnics. Then I took out both Snowdrop and Frost, and we had a lovely picnic in the valley nearby.

Back in the cabin, I started on breakfast. It was eggs I'd bought in town, wild boar sausages I'd made myself, toast, and pancakes with strawberry jam. I loaded everything onto the biggest tray I could find and took it upstairs. Frost looked at me forlornly, but I shook my head, and he went to lie in front of the fire. When I reached the bedroom door, I stopped, waited a beat, then knocked.

"Just a minute!"

Aura sounded cheerful. I heard her footsteps as she padded around the room, then she was right behind the door, and my heart started beating wildly in my chest. I saw the door handle move, and I wondered what would happen if we came face to face now, and she wasn't wearing the mask. I forced myself to stay put. I had to trust her.

She opened the door. She had the mask on. It covered half of her face, and I hated that I couldn't see her eyes. It dawned on me that I had no idea what color they were. I was tempted to tell her to remove it just so I could quench my curiosity, but I thought better of it. She was playing along, still, which meant we could have a nice, quiet day together before she found out I was a legit monster who actually looked like a monster.

I wasn't like those creatures who could shift into men. I'd seen dragons years ago, and while they were massive reptiles who could fly and breathe fire, when they wanted to, they could shift into a form that resembled humans. Wolfmen could shift too, and while they were still hairy as humans, they weren't as hairy as I was. I wished I could take a different shape for Aura.

"Are you hungry?"

"I am. It smells amazing."

She moved out of the doorway, and I walked in. I placed the tray on the bed, then went to her. She'd washed up and put on one of the dresses I'd prepared for her and stored in the closet next to my clothes. Her hair was soft and shiny, and it tumbled down her back in beautiful waves. I took her hand and guided her to the bed. I helped her get in and settle comfortably against the pillows.

"Breakfast in bed," she said. "I haven't had breakfast in bed... mmm... ever!"

I was shocked to learn that. She was so precious, she should've always had breakfast in bed. But then I had to remember that my Aura came from a town that was mostly poor. I knew nothing about her life before, except that she'd asked the priest to give the credits to her best friend, Mina, which meant that she didn't have any family. As I sat down beside her and we ate, I asked her about her parents and if she had any siblings.

"No siblings," she said as she chewed on a piece of sausage I'd fed her. "My parents passed away last year. It was the fever. Some sort of flu that many people in town got. The old and the frail didn't stand a chance. It was a harsh winter, and everyone says this year, it will be even worse. A lot more people are going to die, and I don't even want to think about it. Medicine is hard to come by, and even if I managed to get it for my parents, it did nothing in the end."

"I'm so sorry."

"Thank you. I've made my peace with it. I believe things happen exactly the way they're supposed to. I believe in a higher power, you might say."

"I believe in a higher power, too." The power that had brought us together.

She chuckled, and I was confused at first, because I hadn't said anything funny, but it turned out she was absorbed by her own thoughts.

"It's silly. Because then it means this higher power burned down my house, so I would send my blood to the Temple and be matched with you."

"Your house burned down?"

"Yes. Recently. It was market day, so I wasn't at home. I went to sell the things that I'd knitted. Gloves, socks, scarves... All winter themed, you know. And when I returned home, my house was burning, and my neighbors were trying to put out the fire. I had to move in with Mina and her husband. They're my only friends. I grew up with Mina, and I just can't imagine my life without her. I hope I can see her again sometime, even if I live so far now. I couldn't take advantage of her generosity, though, so I contacted the Temple. So... yeah... that is my story."

I didn't know what to say. Her story was sad. And she was so bright, and beautiful, and happy. She didn't deserve any of it. At a loss for words, I leaned in and kissed the top of her head.

"You knit," I said. "I love knitting too. I also work with leather, and I can make pretty much anything with these two hands, granted they're big and clumsy."

She laughed. "Did you make the dress I'm wearing?"

"Yes."

"Then your hands are anything but clumsy. The stitching is impeccable. I have a lot to learn from you, dear husband."

Dear husband. She said it playfully, like she was joking or teasing me, and I loved it. I could get used to Aura calling me her dear husband.

We finished breakfast when Aura swore she couldn't take another bite. I cleaned up and held the tray in one hand as I guided her toward the door with the other.

"Careful," I said. "Here come the stairs."

She sighed. "Can't you just let me take this off?"

"I'm sorry, not yet."

"Ugh. Let me just take a peek. I'll lift one corner just so I can walk down the stairs without tripping."

"Wait here. I'll take this to the kitchen, then come back for you."

"Seriously?"

She sounded frustrated. Before she could protest, I hurried down the stairs, knowing that with no other option, she would wait for me. Frost greeted me with enthusiasm, then followed me up the stairs to help me bring Aura down. Help me emotionally, that was.

"I'll carry you," I said.

"Fine."

I took her in my arms, and she waited patiently for me to descend the stairs, keeping her hands to herself. Frost followed us, sniffing at her long wool skirt. I set her down, and she stepped away from me only to trip over Frost. She lost her balance, and my hand shot out to grab her by the waist. I thought she would be mad, but she laughed instead, and scratched Frost's head. The dog was so big that his head reached her chest. He was polite enough not to jump on her.

"Oh, you're huge! What breed is he?" she asked me.

"I don't know," I said. "I found him in the woods when he was a puppy. I had no idea he would grow so big."

Aura played with Frost for a few minutes, then I helped her put on her boots and coat, and the three of us went outside. It was chilly but pleasant, and there wasn't a single cloud in the sky. It had snowed the night before, and our boots made satisfying crunching sounds when we walked. A crow cawed in a tree, and Aura whipped her head around, trying to identify where the sound came from.

"Is that Frost's friend?"

"Yes."

"Does he have a name?"

"I haven't thought of giving him a name," I said. "I just call him... crow."

"That needs to change," she declared. "I'll think of a name, okay? It's not just a crow. It's Frost's friend."

I loved that she was so involved in our animals' lives already. And Frost adored her. Usually, he would sniff around me and try to make me play with him, but now he was all over Aura.

We went to visit Snowdrop, and I guided her to him and placed her hands on his neck. They got acquainted properly, and it was nice to hear her talk to the horse like he was a person.

As we walked around the property, I described everything to her. The way the cabin looked from the outside, the stream that came from higher up in the mountain and ran behind the cabin, the trees, the barn, and the greenhouse. We were going to have fresh vegetables all winter because I worked in the greenhouse every day. Today, I sat her down in a corner as I worked, and she was happy to listen to me babble on about my tomatoes and my zucchini. When it was time for lunch, I washed my hands and led her back to the cabin.

"Are you bored?" I asked as I clattered around in the kitchen.

Aura was sitting on the floor with Frost.

"No. I had a lot of fun today. Is it getting dark?"

"Not yet, but it will in an hour or two. The temperature has dropped. We can stay inside after lunch."

"And do... what? Not that I'm bored." She laughed.

"I could read to you."

"Really? What books do you have?"

"Classics, mostly."

I wasn't going to tell her about the dating and relationship books. Before I let her remove her mask, I had to remember to hide them somewhere safe. What would she think of me if she saw them?

"Wuthering Heights," I said. "Or I can read you something more Christmassy, like... A Christmas Carol? Of course, they're both missing chapters."

"Yes, that sounds good. It's a plan!"

We had lunch in the living room, in front of the fire, and I fed her, like usual. Since she had her hands free, she scratched Frost's head throughout lunch, which made him ridiculously happy. Soon, we would have to fight for her attention. It was a good thing Snowdrop didn't live in the cabin with us. He was more of a loner, anyway.

After lunch, Aura made herself comfortable on the couch, and I opened A Christmas Carol and started reading. The fire burned quietly in the fireplace, and the sun started to set. Aura listened attentively, and even Frost settled down at the foot of the couch, but literature was not one of his passions, so he was soon asleep, snoring softly.

I was deep into chapter three when she moved closer to me. I panicked a little, but I also craved her touch, so when she pressed herself against my side, I let her. I was wearing a shirt anyway, so all she could feel was cotton under her fingertips, not my thick fur. Then she shifted again and pushed herself up on her knees and started clumsily climbing on top of me.

I dropped the book.

AURA

He didn't move. As I climbed on top of him, I heard him drop the book. He was frozen, and I took that as my cue to do whatever I pleased.

First, I placed my hands on his chest. The cotton shirt he was wearing was thick, but I could feel that underneath it, his chest was hairy. Furry, almost. Maybe he was covered in hair, maybe in fur... I wondered for a second if that bothered me. I traced my hands upwards until I reached his neck. Where I'd expected to touch skin, there was only more hair. I threaded my fingers through it and concluded that I didn't mind it at all.

"I want you," I said, as my hands found his face. I ran my fingers over his nose, and I found it was long and curved. His lips were soft, and I lifted myself to try to kiss him, but I ended up kissing his jaw. I giggled. "Sorry. I just... I need you."

He grunted, then whispered my name. "Aura..."

I waited for him to say more, but he remained silent. He didn't know how to react, and that gave me a thrill. I made myself more comfortable on his lap, and he let out another strained grunt. I felt him grow hard, and I smiled to myself. I loved that I could do that to him. I rolled my hips teasingly, and he grew even harder. I was starting to make out the shape of his cock as it was trapped between our bodies.

There were too many clothes in the way. I got off him and quickly removed my tights and my panties.

"Don't move," I said as I struggled to get them off as fast as I could.

I was safe, though. Krampus seemed to be in some sort of shock, because he didn't move an inch. I wanted to see the look on his face so badly! I climbed back onto his lap and started working on his belt. I undid it, then I started fiddling with the buttons on his pants.

"I've never done this before," he said.

It was my time to freeze. "What?"

"I've never been with a woman before."

I'd undone three or four buttons by now. I stopped and placed my hands on his shoulders. This conversation was hard to have with my eyes covered. I was at a disadvantage because I had no way of reading his expression.

"But you're... You're old." I cringed. I shouldn't have put it that way. "I mean, older than me."

"I might be older than you and I can imagine," he said, and I identified a hint of regret in his voice.

"What do you mean? Do you not know how old you are?"

"I don't."

"But that... doesn't make any sense."

I stopped what I was doing and settled on his lap. My core throbbed for him, and I wanted to reach between us and touch him, but I held back. This conversation was more important than my sudden lust.

"Aura, I have to tell you something."

"Okay."

"I don't know how old I am, and I also don't know who I am. Presumably, I've been here since before the Shift."

I paled. "But the Shift was so long ago!" We learned about it in history class.

"Yes. When it happened, I lost my memory. Completely. Well, not completely. I could remember this one thing, this one word."

"What's the word?"

"Krampus."

"Oh. Your name."

"That's the thing... I don't know if it's my name or the name of my species. After things settled down and humans and monsters started rebuilding the world, I looked far and wide, trying to find someone like me. I thought... I must have a community too. A clan, a family... something. I found nothing."

"Oh, I'm so sorry." I placed my hands on his face. "I can't even imagine how it must have been for you all this time, living here alone."

"Yes. Well, I got used to it. When I found this place, I fell in love with its beauty. It was isolated, and that was good, because I soon learned that humans were afraid of me. Humans are used to seeing monsters all around them, but those are monsters they know, monsters that... make sense. I was unique, and they never accepted me. When I moved here and built the cabin, the town at the foot of the mountain didn't exist. When humans started building houses and moving in, I wanted to flee at first. Find another place. But then I realized it would be hard to find a place as good as this one, so I stayed. The first time I went into town, I fully expected to be shunned. I expected people to throw rocks at me, but they didn't. They allowed me to walk around and shop in their stores. My credits were just as good as theirs. They let me know immediately that they didn't feel comfortable with me there, but they didn't make me leave. So, I thought... it wasn't so bad. In time, they might come to accept me."

"Did they?" I didn't know why I was asking this question. I already knew the answer.

"No. Not really. They don't bother me, and I don't bother them. They only talk to me if they must. It's fine. I'm grateful they never come near my cabin, because if they wanted to, they could run me out of my own home."

"They would never do that!"

And I believed it. They would make up stories about him, and how he was the monster who ate children if they were naughty, but the townspeople would never be so cruel as to shun Krampus. He'd done nothing to them. It wasn't his fault humans were so fearful and superstitious. I promised myself right then that I would never tell him about the stories they'd made up to scare their kids into behaving. I was most definitely never going to tell him my own parents had used them to make me go to bed early.

"So... now you know," he said.

"But that doesn't mean you've never done this before," I said, letting my hands once again explore his big, muscular chest. I moved lower and lower until I reached his fly and resumed unbuttoning his pants. "You just don't remember. I can't be your first. You're mine. But it's such a stretch to believe I'm yours."

"I don't know, Aura. If I don't remember, then it's like it never happened."

"I guess so..."

Buttons finally undone, I reached inside his pants and touched his cock. Oh my, it was long and thick, and frankly... there was a fair chance it was as big as my arm. I shuddered at the thought. It was going to hurt, but I still wanted him inside me.

"Aura..." He tried to stop me by wrapping his fingers around my wrist.

"Don't you want this? I'm your bride. Don't you want me?"

"I do, but…"

"What?"

He said nothing. I continued to stroke him gently, simply exploring his cock. It felt… unusual. Like nothing I'd expected, for sure. The head was smooth, but the length seemed to be covered in deep ridges. It was also a bit harsh to the touch, like it was covered in the same fur that covered his body, albeit it was sparser here.

"Aura, I don't think…"

"Krampus, just let me…" I shifted on top of him, and when I sat back down, my pussy came in contact with his shaft. If I wanted to position him at my entrance, I would have to lift my hips higher than this. For now, it felt good to just rub myself on him. "This feels amazing. Why are you fighting it?"

"You don't understand…"

He was panting, and I wanted to see his face. I was done with his silly rules and traditions. I was done with the leather mask. Before I could change my mind, and before he caught on to what I wanted to do, I yanked the mask off.

It took a second for my eyes to adjust. It was dark outside, and the only light came from the fireplace. Krampus had his eyes closed and his lips parted, and he didn't notice that I'd taken off my mask. He was so big that even sitting on his lap, I had to look up at his face. And sure enough, it was covered in fur. He was, as I'd guessed, furry from head to toe. The horns on his head were huge, his nose was long and crooked, his cheekbones were high, and his ears stuck upright on the sides of his head, big and pointy.

This was my husband. This was Krampus.

Noticing that I hadn't moved in a while, he slowly opened his eyes. They were as dark as the night.

We stared at each other for a minute, neither of us making a single gesture. His expression didn't change, except for his eyes widening in shock.

And then he did the last thing I'd imagined he'd do.

He pushed me off him.

KRAMPUS

Horror. When she looked at me, I could tell she couldn't stand the sight of me.

For a moment in time, we were both frozen. She in terror, I in wonder. Her eyes were golden. I'd seen nothing like it in humans. There were species on Alia Terra with golden eyes, so I wondered if Aura might've had an ancestor who was not entirely human. After all, since the Temples had been created, monsters took human brides all the time, and Alia Terra was filled with hybrids of all kinds.

As much as I wanted to lose myself in her eyes forever, I felt like I needed to run. And hide. I pushed her off me, and before she understood what was happening and regained her balance, I buttoned up my pants and ran to the door. Frost jumped to his feet, alerted by the commotion, and when I opened the door, he slipped through, and we both found ourselves outside.

I stood in the harsh wind for a second. I'd put on my boots but hadn't laced them up. It wasn't snowing yet, but it felt like it would soon. It felt like a snowstorm was brewing, which was so fitting, because what I felt inside was like a storm.

I looked around me, unsure of what to do next. The only good option seemed to be the barn. I knew I couldn't run from my bride forever, but I needed a few minutes to myself. To think. I headed in that direction, and Frost followed me. Inside, it was warm, and Snowdrop turned his head to greet us.

I closed the door, walked over to Snowdrop to pat him on the back, then sat on the floor, feeling like my legs couldn't carry me anymore. Frost lay his head on my lap, where Aura had been just a few minutes ago.

How perfectly we fit together! Despite the considerable size difference, when she touched me, it felt right. She hadn't seemed terrified. On the contrary, she'd been so eager and confident. But then she'd had to do the one thing I'd asked not to. She'd taken off her mask and looked at my face.

"It's over," I said to Snowdrop, who was eating his hay lazily and looking at me. "She'll want to leave now. She didn't say it, but I could see it in her eyes.

She thinks I'm hideous. I don't blame her. I think I'm hideous."

Snowdrop sighed heavily. If he could talk, what would he say? Would he comfort me?

I looked down at Frost, and he looked up at me with his huge eyes. When he looked at me like that, I saw a puppy, not a massive beast who could scare the people in town with one bark.

"No woman would ever want to be with me. Not even her, who was chosen for me by the Temple. She couldn't even speak when she saw me. She's always so chatty, but when she took off the mask, she was speechless. I waited for her to say something, and when she didn't, I couldn't be there anymore, in the same room, with her so close to me. Now that she knows who I am, what I look like... she'll never touch me again. I'll be lucky if she still wants to speak to me."

Neither Snowdrop nor Frost said anything. They only communicated with their eyes, and I could tell they felt sorry for me. It had only been two days. Two days of pure bliss, and starting tomorrow, I was going to be alone again. Eternally alone, because I wasn't going to try taking a bride a second time.

"I should go back and talk to her," I said. "She probably wants to go back home today. It's dark outside, but I'm sure you can navigate these roads with your eyes closed," I said to Snowdrop. He nodded. Or I chose to think he did. I scratched Frost behind the ears. "Do you want to come with us? I know you like her. She likes you too. I think she'll miss you. She won't miss me, but she'll miss you, for sure."

I was just about to get off the floor and face reality when there was a knock on the barn door. Great. Reality had come to face me.

"Krampus? Are you in there?"

I flopped back down, my legs once again refusing to do what they were supposed to do.

"Stupid question," she continued. "I know you're in there because I followed your footprints." Another beat. "I'm coming in."

"No!"

Too late. She was done listening to me. The door opened, and she walked inside. At least it was dark enough that she couldn't see my face clearly. I could see her – her rosy cheeks, her full lips, her golden eyes and auburn hair – and I felt the urge to walk over to her and take her in my arms. She had her winter boots on, and her coat, but no gloves, scarf, or hat. It was a good thing the barn was heated.

"What are you doing in here?" she asked. "Why did you leave like that?"

She stepped closer to me, and I had to stop her.

"That's close enough," I said.

She frowned. "Why are you doing this, Krampus?"

She didn't advance, though, and I was grateful. The look on her face told me she was feeling frustrated with me. Annoyed. She didn't avert her gaze, which made me feel hopeful that, after all, maybe she wasn't that terrified of me. Back in the cabin, she'd looked shocked. Now she seemed calm and collected, and maybe the simple fact that she'd come searching for me was a good sign.

What could I tell her? There were so many answers to her question, all viable.

"No more lies," she insisted. "I want to know why you're behaving this way. I know you lied about the mask. You just told me you lost your memory, and the only thing you remembered after the Shift was your name. So, you have no idea what your traditions were before the Shift. You made up that thing about the leather mask. It's time for you to fess up and tell me why."

A pause.

"Or this marriage won't work."

AURA

I hated that I had to be so harsh to him, but I was done playing games. I wanted to start our life together already. I wanted to make this place my home, but we couldn't build a firm foundation if we couldn't trust each other.

"Okay, I will tell you," he said after a long pause. "But please... can you not look at me?"

"What do you mean?"

"Just... don't look directly at me."

He covered his face with his hand. I frowned. What was he on about? This was ridiculous! But if I wanted to get something out of him, then I had to meet him halfway.

"All right."

I studied the floor and chose a spot to sit down. The barn was spotless, and it was heated too, which was impressive. The way he treated his horse and his dog said a lot about Krampus, and it was one reason why I wanted this to work out. He had a good heart. As I sat down, I slightly turned away from him. I could see him from the corner of my eye.

"Is this good?" I asked.

"Yes. Thank you."

"No problem."

He took a deep breath, released it slowly, then started talking.

"You're right, Aura. I lied to you, and I feel ashamed. There is no tradition that says the bride should have her eyes covered on the wedding day. Or after. I made it up because I didn't know what to do." He let out a heavy groan, as if he were in pain. "Look at me! How could I let you see me? You wouldn't have even made it to the altar. One glance at me, and you would've turned around and left straight through the front door of the Temple."

"You don't know that."

"I know how the townspeople look at me when I come down to stock up on food. When I enter the store, they leave within minutes, and I can tell the store clerks want to leave too, but they can't. People gather outside and look at me through the windows, whisper among themselves, and when they see I'm paying for my groceries and getting ready to walk out, they disperse."

"I'm sorry..."

"It's okay. It's not your fault. It's mine. Because I look like this."

"Krampus, listen..."

But he wasn't done. "I know what they say about me. That I'm ugly. That I'm the scariest creature they've ever seen. They tell their children that if they're not nice, Krampus will come get them and do unspeakable things to them."

I bit the inside of my lip. I wanted to tell him that was not true, but unfortunately, it was. Though, "unspeakable things" was a bit of a stretch. Or... was it? The story said that Krampus would eat you if you were naughty. Okay, so cannibalism was definitely not a stretch.

It was awful that I couldn't contradict him on anything he was saying. Right now, I felt ashamed of my town.

"So, you see, I couldn't let you see me on our wedding day. I couldn't risk having my heart broken when you turned away. I fully intended to let you remove the mask once we got to the cabin, but then everything was going so well, and I loved being with you, and I thought... What if you kept your eyes covered a little bit longer? What if I didn't let you see me, didn't let you touch me at all, and you didn't know who I was and what I looked like, and what if, eventually, you would like me for me, and then... and then maybe it wouldn't matter that I was so ugly?"

"Oh, Krampus..."

I'd suspected this was the reason he'd made me wear the mask and tied my hands at night. Still, his confession came like a gut punch. As he spoke, he kept half of his face covered with his hand and didn't look at me. It hurt to see him like this. I wanted to go to him, so I shifted on my hands and knees and started slowly crawling toward him.

"No. You promised you'd keep your distance and not look directly at me."

I rolled my eyes. "Krampus, I'm your wife! We did... things. We share a bed!"

"Yes, but now you know that I'm a monster. A real monster, not like one of those who're handsome, even if they have beastly features."

"Okay, listen." I was in front of him now, and I plopped back down on the floor. Frost moved his big head from his lap to mine. "I don't believe you're ugly. What you look like doesn't matter to me at all. What matters is your heart. How you treat me, how you treat Frost, Snowdrop, and just... everyone."

He looked at me reluctantly. "Thank you for saying that, but..."

"But what?"

"You're so beautiful, Aura. Someone like you could never love someone like me. You deserve better."

"Ugh!" I was losing my patience.

"Even if the DNA test said we are a perfect match... The truth is that I looked at us in the mirror, the way we look together, next to each other, and we're such a perfect... mismatch. You deserve to be with someone who is beautiful, like you."

"Seriously? You're going to decide that for me? I told you: I don't care. Looks don't matter. What I care about is the way you treat me, the way you love me and take care of me. And Krampus, no one has ever taken care of me like you did these past two days."

He lowered his gaze and shook his head, then covered his face with both hands. I waited for him to say something, but he remained silent. What did that mean? That the conversation was over?

This was so frustrating! No matter what I said, he only heard what he wanted to. He was stuck in his idea that he was hideous and I deserved something better. How was I supposed to change his mind when he didn't want to let me in?

"Krampus, you have to believe me when I say that you are exactly what I need," I tried again.

"But I'm not what you want…"

My mouth opened and closed. Was I not saying the right things? What were the right things to say?

"I want you. And there's no way you can doubt that after what we just did in the cabin. Or tried to do before you freaked out and ran."

I was referring to my climbing on top of him. I'd removed my panties and tights, and when he rushed out of the house and I followed him, I'd only had time to put on the panties. I hoped I wouldn't come to regret it soon. The barn was cozy, but it sounded like a snowstorm was brewing outside.

"I'm sorry, Aura. It doesn't make any sense. It's hard to believe that someone like you…"

"Ugh!" With that, I jumped to my feet. Startled, Frost crawled away from me. "You're infuriating! Everything I tell you goes right past your head. If you want to stay here and mope, fine. I told you how I feel, and I'm done arguing with you."

I turned on my heel and stomped toward the door. Before walking out, I threw one last look over my shoulder. He was still there, sitting with his shoulders hunched, looking sad and defeated. I couldn't deal with it. I stormed out of the barn and shut the door behind me.

I couldn't deal with the fact that everything he'd said about how the townspeople had been treating him was true, and deep down, I understood a few words from me would not change his mind about humans. I was one of them, so he struggled to believe that someone who belonged to a species that had only shown contempt toward him could love him and want to be with him.

I didn't know what to do. I was at a loss, and he wasn't letting me in. I wrapped my arms around myself and started walking toward the cabin. The wind was blowing hard, making a mess of my hair. It was snowing heavily, and I could barely see a few feet in front of me. The moon was full and high in the sky, providing just enough light for me to not get lost.

The cabin wasn't far. The light, as diffused as it was, gave me a feeling of comfort. The time to regret not putting my tights on was now. My legs were literally freezing, and my boots barely came up to my knees. It was a good thing my dress was thick and made of wool, and I also had my coat. A hat wouldn't have hurt... Oh well.

Between the barn and the cabin, I got distracted by the beauty of the landscape. I knew this was a bad time, but I couldn't help straying from the path just a little. I wanted to see the mountain spring that ran behind the cabin. It was going to take only a minute, and if I hurried, I wasn't going to freeze.

Behind the cabin, the woods spread up the mountain, dark and ominous. The stream was tiny and nearly frozen. The moonlight's reflection in the water made it look like it was peppered with diamonds. It was such a beautiful sight that I almost forgot the argument I'd had with Krampus. It wasn't that bad, after all. He just needed a few more minutes to himself to think about what I'd said to him. When he was ready, he would find me in the cabin, warming up by the fire, and we'd have a laugh about it.

I walked upstream for a bit, then decided it was time to turn back. The storm had intensified, and if I didn't go back now, I had a feeling I wouldn't be able to see the cabin anymore. I tried to hurry, but the snow was so thick and soft that every step I took was a struggle. I was making progress, though, so I wasn't worried.

Until I saw movement in the snow, a few feet to my left.

Something tiny, well camouflaged in the white landscape, and moving much faster than me. In the opposite direction.

When I understood what it was, I knew I had to catch it.

KRAMPUS

Could it be true? Could it be that Aura didn't care how I looked and could see past it? Every time we touched, I could feel that she wanted me just as much as I wanted her. And even though she was shocked when she took off her mask and saw me for the first time, when she came into the barn to talk to me, she behaved totally normally.

She'd walked out a few minutes ago, maybe ten, maybe twenty, and I was feeling better. I was ready to go back to the cabin and face her in full light. I got up, made sure Snowdrop had everything he needed for the night, then left the barn with Frost in tow. The snowstorm was in full swing. Even with my perfect sight, it was hard to see a few feet in front of me. I held my head down and made my way to the cabin.

"Aura?"

I took off my coat and boots and stalked into the living room. She wasn't there. She wasn't in the kitchen either, and when I knocked on the bathroom door, there was no answer. I frowned and went to look for her upstairs, feeling uneasy. After five minutes of searching for her, I was downright scared. Her things were still here, but that meant nothing. If she got mad at me and wanted to leave, she would leave without her few belongings just to put distance between us as fast as possible. In this snowstorm, she wouldn't be able to carry a bag, anyway.

I got dressed and rushed outside. Frost was with me, barking and running around me, as if to ask me what the plan was.

"We have to find her," I said. "She can't have gone far."

I looked around for footprints, but it was snowing so heavily that even my own footprints from a few minutes before had been covered. I cursed under my breath and started on the path that led to town. It was the only thing that made sense. Aura had been angry when she'd left the barn, and in her anger, maybe she decided to punish me by going home.

"Come on, Frost. Help me."

He immediately put his nose to work. We walked for a while, and I called her name a few times, hoping she would hear me.

"Aura! Where are you? If you can hear me, please come back. I'll take you back into town tomorrow, I promise!"

What had I done? She'd been so nice to me. She'd told me she liked me for who I was and didn't care about my looks, and I'd pushed her away. I was such an idiot! So many dating and relationships books read, and for nothing. The first chance I got, I ruined it all. I wasn't good with people, which made sense since I'd been alone for so long, but still... I could've made an effort.

Now she was pissed off, and for good reason. Had I been in her shoes – or boots – I wouldn't have wanted to have anything to do with me either. Back there, in the barn, I'd been difficult. I shouldn't have let her leave. What was I thinking, letting her walk out in this menace of a storm?

I hoped she was okay. It occurred to me that I hadn't looked in the greenhouse, and that made me stop in my tracks. I turned on my heel and saw that

Frost wasn't by my side anymore. I shielded my eyes from the snow and tried to see where he was.

"Frost?"

Great. The last thing I needed tonight was to lose my dog, too. I was terrible at forming and keeping relationships, it appeared.

"Frost! Where are you?"

A bark from up ahead told me he hadn't abandoned me.

"What are you doing there?"

At first, I thought he was smarter than me and realized Aura had been in the greenhouse all along, but then I saw he wasn't headed to the greenhouse. He'd strayed from the path that led to town and was barking and jumping to make me follow him behind the cabin.

But there was nothing behind the cabin. Just the stream that ran down from the mountain, and the dark, dense woods. Why would Aura ever go there? There was nothing to see. It was even dangerous if you didn't know these parts.

"Frost, wait for me!"

What was I supposed to do? He was a good, loyal dog, and his nose never betrayed him. He liked Aura, and he'd never let anything happen to her.

"Okay, boy. Let's find her."

AURA

I hadn't realized I'd gone so far. I followed the tiny creature until I found myself in the woods. The ball of fluff was nearly frozen when I caught it. It tried to run away from me, thinking I was a predator, but the snow was too much even for it, and it couldn't advance further. I took it in my hands and looked at its cute little face. It was the most adorable baby bunny I'd ever seen.

"Where is your mommy?" I asked, my teeth chattering. I could barely speak, not that the bunny could understand me. "How did you get so lost?" Then I looked around me and shook my head. "Now we're both lost. But at least we have each other."

A scarf would've been welcome. And a hat, and the tights that I'd left abandoned on the floor of the living room. I couldn't feel my knees. I tucked the baby rabbit underneath my coat, close to my heart, and it latched onto me, happy it had found some warmth. By now, it knew I wasn't going to hurt it. As I held it there with care, I looked around me, trying to make out the cabin in the distance. On a bright day, I would've been able to see it, but it was dark, the moon had hidden behind the clouds, and the snow wasn't letting up.

"We have to move," I said to the bunny. "And keep moving, or we'll freeze to death."

I started in the direction I thought would lead me to the cabin. I looked for my own footprints in the snow, but the wind and the snowfall had covered them. It was hard to see, and it was hard to walk. I tripped on something, regained my balance, then took a deep breath and instantly regretted it. It hurt to breathe. Heavy snowflakes clung to my hair, my eyebrows and eyelashes, and I was shaking so hard from the cold that I could barely stand upright. I tried to relax and will my body to adapt to the constantly dropping temperature, telling myself that it was fine, I hadn't gone too far, and the cabin or the barn would soon come into view.

I started to lose feeling in my toes, but I pushed on. Against my chest, the baby bunny was warm and comfortable. If not for that, I would've been really pissed at myself right now that I'd been so irresponsible.

Soon enough, I saw something before me. It was tall and shadowy, but it was something, so I hurried toward it.

"Krampus!" I called.

I couldn't distinguish any clear features, and I got closer and closer, until I literally walked into a tree. I would've laughed, had I not hurt my head pretty badly. I felt like crying, but if I did, my tears would turn into icicles, and that would definitely not improve my situation.

"Stupid," I said to myself.

The tree was tall, with a thick trunk. I couldn't believe I'd mistaken it for Krampus. Was he even looking for me? Did he know I was gone? I'd left him in the barn after he'd annoyed me with his silly pity party, and now I felt bad for having done that to him. I'd told him that I needed and wanted him, and my actions from earlier in the day had proven it. What else did he want me to say? Why couldn't he just believe me?

I slid to the ground, using the tree as support. It somewhat protected me from the snow. I was so tired that I didn't think I could take another step. I was going to rest here for a moment, then get up and find the cabin.

Thinking about Krampus, I felt differently now. I wasn't annoyed anymore, and I could see I'd been wrong to not give him time to process my words and get used to the idea that I liked him just the way he was. I couldn't blame him for not believing me. The townspeople had been so mean to him, and I'd grown up in that community. Surely, he thought the stories about him had influenced me.

And they had, to some extent. But then I met him and saw how kind and generous he was, and suddenly, those stories meant nothing at all. They were just silly things told by silly people who were afraid of the unknown. I wasn't like that. I wasn't afraid of the unknown, otherwise I wouldn't have sent my blood to the Temple to be mated to a monster. I was glad it was Krampus.

No, it didn't matter to me at all that he was big and covered in fur, that he had horns, and that he wasn't handsome in the way a human would expect. What if he was handsome for his own species? He was the only survivor, so we would never know, but who cared? I didn't. It had only been two days, and I already felt attached to him.

I loved spending time with him, talking to him, and I adored his cooking. I loved how gentle and careful he was with me, and that he wanted me to be warm and comfortable at all times. Well, except for that one time when he tied my hands to the bed, but I wasn't going to hold that one exception against him. And the leather mask had pissed me off too, but maybe it hadn't been too bad that he'd made me wear it. It forced me to slow down and let someone else take control.

I curled up, trying to preserve some heat. I could feel the baby bunny's heart beating steadily next to mine, and I wondered if it was asleep. I was feeling beyond exhausted. I didn't want to close my eyes, but I had to because the wind was too harsh.

"One more minute," I whispered to myself. "I'll rest my eyes for one minute, then I'm getting up."

Never mind that I couldn't feel anything below the waist. Somehow, I was going to make it.

I must have dozed off. I woke up with a start and tried to move my limbs, but nothing seemed to work. I checked on the bunny rabbit, and he was sleeping peacefully against my chest. That gave me hope. I struggled to push myself to my feet, but it was no use. I only managed to end up on my knees. My dress was soaked, and I couldn't feel my nose, my lips, my ears... nothing. It was like... I knew I had a face, but I couldn't feel it.

"Okay, I just need to rest a bit more. I'm weak, but I'll feel stronger in a minute."

I dozed off again, and this time, I was woken up by a noise. No, a voice. It sounded low and guttural, and when I opened my eyes, I saw a massive shadow standing over me.

"Krampus?" I whispered. Or tried to. In truth, I probably didn't make a sound, and just called his name in my head.

I looked up, up, up... and was met with the sight of two incandescent eyes. They burned in the sheer darkness like the eyes of a beast.

Despite myself, I screamed.

Krampus

Her reaction to seeing me hurt me deeply. It was a miracle I'd found her, and it was all thanks to Frost and his sharp nose. But when I called her name, and she looked up at me and screamed, my heart shattered in my chest. I took a step back, then I saw her collapse on her side. I rushed to catch her. She was limp in my arms, and I realized she'd fainted. From the cold or as a result of seeing me... I didn't know. I gathered her in my arms and motioned to Frost to lead the way. In this snowstorm, I couldn't quite see the cabin myself.

What had she been thinking? I'd have expected her to take the road to town, not go behind the cabin and into the woods. I'd found her at the edge of the woods, sleeping with her back against a tree.

I looked down at her as Frost and I approached the cabin. Her pale skin had turned blue, and her beautiful lips were purple. She was breathing evenly, her eyes moving underneath her lids. I couldn't believe one look at my face in the dark had caused her to faint!

Maybe I shouldn't have jumped to conclusions. She was nearly frozen and exhausted. She couldn't control her limbs in these circumstances, so how would she be able to control her reaction to being rescued? I would find out the truth soon enough. What was important now was that she was safe. I needed to get her inside, run her a warm bath, and hope her toes and fingers were intact. Hypothermia was no joke. Even I was suffering in this horrible weather, and I was a monster that was covered in fur from head to toe, and also, quite possibly, immortal.

I pushed the door to the cabin open, and Frost shot inside. Right in the middle of the entry hall, he shook off all the snow that had gathered in his fur. I couldn't blame him. Frost liked the snow, but not when it was as menacing as it was tonight. He padded into the living room, plopped his butt in front of the fire, and proceeded to scratch his ear.

I felt Aura stir in my arms, and I hurried to lay her down on the couch. I didn't want her to wake up in my arms, with her face so close to my face, and risk having her faint again. Once she was comfortable with a pillow under her head, I took off my coat and my boots, then I took off her boots and inspected her toes. Fortunately, they looked fine, though a little purple.

"Krampus?" she groaned, sitting up. "Where am I?"

"You're home," I said. "I mean, you're at the cabin," I quickly amended, in case she didn't consider this place her home.

"What happened?" She touched her temple with her trembling fingers, then let out a yelp and both her hands went to her chest. "Oh, he's alive."

"What?" My ears perked. "Who's alive?"

From inside her coat, she pulled out a small bundle of fluff. It was a tiny rabbit.

"I saw him in the snow. He was lost, and I wanted to save him," Aura said.

The bunny rabbit fit perfectly in her hand. I ran a hand through my hair and groaned.

"You followed a rabbit into the woods?"

"He was lost," she said again, her golden eyes fixed on me. "He could've died."

And that was when I understood she hadn't followed the creature like a hunter would, with dinner in mind. She wanted to keep it as a pet. I couldn't suppress another groan. She'd almost died because of a rabbit! On the other hand, did that mean...

"Wait, you didn't want to leave?" I asked.

"Leave? Leave where?"

"Go back home, to your town."

She cocked an eyebrow. "Why would I do that?"

"Because..." But I couldn't finish the sentence. It didn't feel productive to have the same conversation we'd had in the barn.

"Oh, stop it!" She sat up, placed the bunny in her lap, and reached for my hand. "Krampus, I don't want to leave. I'm your wife. I'm going to say this one more time, and then you need to do something about how bloody frozen I am. Okay, here it goes. You ready?"

She took my hand in both her hands and stared right into my eyes. I found I could not look away from her.

"I want you. Because I like you. Just the way you are. It's only been two days, and a relationship needs time, but I think we're on the right track. You take care of me, you cook for me, you treat me like I'm the most important person in the world."

"You are..."

"You make me feel special. And... did you know? Only someone who is special himself can make someone else feel special. We were made for each other. I believe the priest didn't lie at all. The DNA test never gets it wrong. At least in our case, it didn't get it wrong. I'm so happy we found each other."

I swallowed heavily. I had to wait a beat, or my voice would crack if I tried to speak too soon. She'd already seen me broken back in the barn. I wanted to be strong for her.

"Aura... I... I love you."

Her beautiful golden eyes widened, then her whole face relaxed into a smile. She leaned in, and I met her halfway. She hooked one arm around my neck and pulled herself up, while I had to bend over to reach her. Our lips met for the first time.

The kiss was delicate, almost chaste. I didn't dare to do what I wanted, which was to pull her onto my lap and wrap my arms around her, grab her by the back of her neck, and ravish her mouth until she couldn't breathe anymore. Heat bloomed in my chest, moved down to my stomach, then rushed between my legs. I was so hard that it was almost painful. And we weren't even doing anything.

She pulled away and giggled at the bunny in her lap.

"Careful with this one. We don't want to crush him," she said.

Right. The bunny rabbit. I only hoped Frost would accept him, because, like me, he thought rabbits were food.

"Let me put him somewhere safe," I said.

Aura handed the fluff ball to me, and I went to find him a spot in the kitchen. The irony! I put him in a box and placed the box high on the kitchen counter, where Frost couldn't reach him. Just in case. On second thought, I also gave the bunny a carrot to keep him busy, lest he got out of his box and started hopping around the house.

"I'll run you a bath," I told Aura.

"Take me upstairs?"

There were two bathrooms in the house, one downstairs and one upstairs, and they were both big, with massive tubs. Truth be told, I usually washed

Frost in the downstairs tub. I took Aura in my arms once more, and she clung to me.

Once upstairs, she watched me prepare the bath for her. I made sure the water wasn't too hot, since it wouldn't do her any good in the near frozen state she was in, and poured rose oil in the tub. I'd bought it especially for her, and I remembered even now the look the cashier gave me when I paid. Some things would be stuck in my memory forever. Too bad I couldn't remember anything from before the Shift. I liked to believe that my past life had been a pleasant one, with more people in it, people who looked like me.

"Ready?" I asked Aura.

She nodded and stood up, wobbly on her feet.

"Help me?"

I took off her coat, then helped her out of the dress. All her clothes were soaked, down to her bra and panties, and her skin was cold and deathly pale. All I wanted was to take a step back and stare at her naked form, admire her like one would admire a goddess, but there was no time for such things. I had to delay my own needs and desires, because warming her up was the priority. She looked ghostly, like she was with one foot in the world of the living, and the other in the world of the dead.

She was thin and frail, but her curves were enticing. Her hourglass figure made her the most beautiful woman I'd ever seen. I hated it that it was always so cold here and she had to hide her body underneath layers of cotton, wool, and fur. In our bedroom, I was going to crank up the heat, and hopefully... I would be able to see more of her, more often.

"I don't think I can get in on my own," she said, standing in front of the tub.

"You don't have to."

Gently, I lifted her up and lowered her into the rising water. It came up to just below her round, incredible breasts, and it was hard to look away. Her nipples were hard and dark pink, and all I wanted was to touch them, take them into my mouth and tease them slowly. My cock was so hard by now that I needed to readjust it in my leather pants. I did so discreetly.

Aura hugged her knees to her chest.

"Is the bunny okay?" she asked, waiting for the water to rise and engulf her up to her shoulders.

"Yes. I put him in a box."

"I think I'll name him Fluffy. What do you think?"

I chuckled as I sat next to the tub. "Fitting." I took water in my hands and poured it down her back.

She shuddered. "That feels nice."

"Do you want me to wash your hair?"

"Okay."

We were both silent as I washed her long auburn hair, massaging her scalp until she closed her eyes and let me support her head. She uncurled her body and relaxed.

"Are you still cold?"

"No."

I washed her shoulders and her back next, then she gave me one leg, and I lathered it with soap. I didn't need to use a cloth or a bath sponge, since my hands were huge and covered in hair. She looked at me from behind her long lashes. She was almost asleep.

"You screamed when you saw me," I blurted out. It had weighed heavily on my chest since I'd found her.

"What?"

"You screamed. In the woods, when you saw me."

"Oh. Your eyes. I didn't know they glow in the dark."

"I scared you."

"No, you just took me by surprise. I mean, not you... Your eyes. Does it mean you can see in the dark?"

"Yes. Perfectly."

"That's nice. I wish I could see in the dark..."

"So... I didn't scare you?"

Her eyes snapped open. She sat up and pulled her leg free.

"No. Krampus, you didn't scare me. I was waiting for you. I hoped you would find me."

"I thought you'd left, but then Frost caught your scent..."

"I don't want to hear you say that again," she said firmly. "That you think I would leave you. I will prove to you that I mean it when I say that I want you."

"How?"

She straightened her back and wrung out her wet hair. "Give me a towel. No, two. I need one for my hair."

I did as she requested, and she stood up, letting the water run down her luscious body. I was lost for a moment, not knowing what to do. It was as if my brain refused to work when she was naked in front of me.

"Krampus."

"Yes, here."

I wrapped her in a big, soft towel while she dried her hair.

"Now, take me to our bedroom," she said.

My heart started galloping in my chest.

AURA

I snuggled close to him as he carried me to our bed. I was wrapped in only a towel, but his body gave off enough heat to keep me warm. The room was warm too, almost hot. He wanted to tuck me into bed, but I clung to his arm and pulled him on top of me.

"Stop teasing me," I said. "Just take me."

"Are you sure?"

His voice was deep and low. It made my core vibrate with need.

"Yes," I said.

"Aren't you cold? Does anything hurt? Maybe you're hungry."

I rolled my eyes and wrapped my arms around his neck.

"I said I was going to prove to you that I mean it when I say I want you and need you. Let me prove it to you, Krampus."

With that, I locked our lips in a heated kiss. It felt like he was still reluctant, so I took charge and pushed my tongue into his mouth to meet his. He let out a growl from deep inside his chest, and finally, he took me in his arms and positioned himself between my legs. The towel had slipped off when he got me into bed, and I was naked. But he wasn't. I started pulling at his clothes.

"Take these off," I said.

He got off the bed and quickly slipped out of his shirt and pants. My eyes traveled down his body.

Underneath all that brown fur, he was thick and muscular. He could keep me warm all night. The only thing that worried me was... between his legs. His cock was long, dark, and fully erect. It was so heavy that it had trouble fighting gravity and standing perfectly straight. I licked my lips in anticipation, but at the same time... I wasn't sure it was going to go so well. For one, I was a virgin. And two, the size difference seemed like a real obstacle.

"I'll be gentle," he said, noticing my hesitation. "We don't have to go all the way."

"No, I want to..."

"If it hurts, I'll stop."

I nodded, and he climbed back on top of me.

"Wait," I said. "Can I..." I felt myself blush hard. "Um... Can I taste it?"

Because he'd tasted me, and I felt like I had to return the favor at some point. It wasn't even that. I wanted to see what he tasted like.

"Only if you want to," he said.

"I do."

He rolled onto his back and allowed me to move down his body until my mouth hovered over the glistening tip. The length of his cock rested on his stomach, and when I ran my fingertips over it, his entire shaft twitched upward to meet my touch. The only smooth part of his cock was the head. The length was covered in ridges and hair, and his balls were big and so hairy that when I cupped them with my hand, my fingers completely disappeared into the hair. He let out a groan, and my pussy throbbed and gushed. I didn't know about other women, but it seemed that I was into hairy men. Or monsters.

He was so thick that I had to take hold of his cock with both hands. I guided the tip to my lips, and my tongue darted out for a tentative lick. He tasted sweet and a bit tangy, and I went in for more, this time taking the mushroom head in my mouth and sucking it gently.

"Aura..."

I hummed and took more of him into my mouth, even though my jaw started to protest. It was impossible to take all of him in. Maybe a quarter of his cock fit before I felt the tip poke deep into my throat, too deep for it to feel comfortable anymore. I stopped and sucked as well as I could, licking the underside of his length, bobbing my head up and down, trying to fit one more inch as I relaxed my throat.

"That feels incredible," he whispered.

I looked up at him and met his gaze. I hadn't expected him to be staring at me as I sucked his cock, but he was. My cheeks flushed bright red. I felt hot all over, and I was sure my juices had soaked the sheets already. He was looking at me with hooded eyes. His lips were slightly parted, and he let out small moans and groans as I sucked and licked harder. I wasn't sure what the goal was. I just wanted to make him feel good, and I loved the way he reacted to what I was doing. If he came into my mouth, considering the size of his balls, I was pretty certain I would choke. Besides, I wanted him to come inside me.

The more I thought about it, the more I realized I wanted to taste his cum. Maybe just a little bit...

"Aura... if you continue like this..."

I felt it was fine to take a break. My jaw was killing me.

"What will happen if I continue like this?" I asked.

"I can barely hold back..."

"So, don't."

"I don't know if that's a good idea..."

I didn't know either. I kept stroking him with both hands. His length was slick with my saliva and my hands were gliding easily.

"I want to taste you. Will you give me just a little bit?"

He let out the deepest, most animalistic groan I'd heard from him.

"I don't think that's an option," he said.

"Please try?"

He pursed his lips, but then nodded. "Only if you let me do it." His hand reached between his legs.

"Mmm... okay."

I let go of his cock, and he took charge as I sat up. He sat up too, and because of the size difference, his pelvis ended up in front of my face. I placed my hands on his thick thighs as he pumped his cock, aiming the tip at my lips.

"Open up," he said. "I won't give you all that I have. Just a sip."

The way he said it... My walls clenched and unclenched, and I felt the urge to touch myself. I rubbed myself on the sheets, but the friction wasn't enough.

I parted my lips, and he gently fed me the head of his cock. A few more tugs, and I felt hot liquid drip into my mouth. He let out a long moan, and I could tell he was holding back as best as he could. His face looked strained. I hadn't even thought it was possible for a man to come in such a controlled manner, but he wasn't a man, was he?

"More?" he asked.

I looked up into his eyes and nodded my head. As he pumped his cock a few more times, I cupped his balls with my hand and massaged them slowly. His cum was delicious. I could drink from his cock for as long as he let me, but I could tell it was hard for him to keep this up.

"Aura... I can't..." he said. "I have to... I have to fill you now, or I'll explode."

I pulled away and licked my lips. His eyes were dark and lustful, and his cock was still dripping, even if my mouth wasn't there to catch his cum. He flipped me onto my stomach before I realized what was happening. I yelped, then giggled, then let out a moan when he started penetrating me. I tried to hold myself up on my hands and knees, but the sensation of being filled for the first time was overwhelming. Krampus had to hold me up, because I couldn't do a thing. It was as if my own body refused to listen to me.

The tip was in, and it already felt like too much. He moved in and out of me, with each thrust making my pussy take another inch, then another, until I felt like I was stretched to my absolute limit.

"I can't..." I said, panting heavily. "This is all I can take. Please..."

"Shh... It's okay. This is enough."

He pulled out, then pushed back in. Maybe half of his cock was inside me, and I felt bad for not being able to accommodate all of him, but this was my first time, and it was a miracle I wasn't writhing in pain. It burned a little, but my pussy was so soaked and ready – and mentally, I just wanted him, all of him – that the little pain I felt instantly turned to pleasure.

I let him do all the work. At this point, I was such a mess that not even my brain worked, let alone my limbs. I would've loved to move my hips, let him know how enthusiastic I was about this, but it would have to wait until next time, when I wouldn't feel so overwhelmed with sensations I'd never felt before. My body was just proving to me it was capable of unbridled pleasure, and all I could do was focus on my breathing and on the way my husband's cock moved inside me, in and out, in and out, until the pressure I felt in my pussy grew and burst into an orgasm that almost caused me to faint.

I let out a long scream as I clung to the sheets and pillows. My pussy throbbed around his cock, and soon enough, I heard him let out a growl as he shot his seed deep inside me.

"Hold still," he said. "Hold still, my Aura."

That made me chuckle, because it wasn't like I could move. In fact, I was pretty sure I'd be unable to walk for at least twenty-four hours.

"I need... I need to give you everything I have..."

We stayed like that for minutes on end, him pump-ing his seed inside me. I could feel it coat my walls and go past my cervix, right into my womb. There was so much of it that I soon felt it spill out, and Krampus was still not done. He'd held back when he came into my mouth, and now he wasn't going to hold back one bit.

"My wife," he said. "I love you."

"I love you too."

It felt right to say it. I knew we'd only been married for two days, but we were meant for each other, and there was no doubt in my mind that things were as they should be.

Finally, he was done. With a groan, he pulled out of me, and I felt empty, and then even emptier when his seed rushed out and soaked the sheets. He lay down beside me and gathered me in his arms. I was glistening with sweat, and he felt hot against my damp skin, but I wouldn't have had it any other way. I knew we needed to wash, but there was no way I could get up after what we'd just done.

"You're perfect," he whispered in my ear. "I hope I didn't hurt you."

"You didn't. It's too bad I'm too small for you."

"You're the perfect size."

I laughed. "No, I'm not. But hey, maybe with time... who knows? I'll adapt to your... um... size." I yawned, feeling exhausted.

"Sleep, my beautiful."

He didn't have to tell me twice.

KRAMPUS

My Aura fell asleep in my arms. I couldn't sleep, though. I knew she didn't believe that I was a virgin, but since I couldn't remember having ever been with a female, to me, it felt like the truth. I liked the idea of Aura being my first.

I watched her sleep for an hour, then she stirred in my arms, turned around, and snuggled against my chest. Her face was pressed to my heart, and I was afraid she might not be able to breathe. She slept for another hour, then started fussing again, as if she couldn't find a comfortable position. She opened her eyes, and our gazes met.

"Why aren't you sleeping?" she asked.

"I can't sleep. All I want to do is look at you."

"You were watching me sleep?" She blushed. "A ww... I don't know what to say to that."

"Are you cold?"

"No." Her stomach rumbled then, and she gave me a sheepish smile. "I'm hungry, though."

"I'll bring you something to eat."

"I'll come with you. I want to see Fluffy."

For a second, I didn't know who Fluffy was. Then I remembered the baby rabbit that had gotten her lost. I didn't know how to feel about the creature. She loved it, though, so I had to pretend at least, and hope I'd come to care about it once I got to know it better. Aura had made the choice to follow it and rescue it. I had to remember it wasn't exactly its fault she had almost died of hypothermia.

"All right," I said.

I helped her up, and she held on to me when her knees almost gave out. She giggled, then forced herself to stand upright. I could see my seed spill down the inside of her beautiful legs, and I felt proud. I'd marked her as my own. It was entirely possible that we'd made a baby tonight.

"I have to wash first," she said. "You go ahead and make us something to eat. It will be the last time, by the way. Starting tomorrow, I want to cook."

I frowned. "So, I won't be allowed to cook for you anymore?"

"Occasionally," she said.

"But I love cooking."

"You can cook for Frost, then. I love cooking too. When was the last time someone cooked for you, Krampus?"

She started toward the bathroom, and I found myself mesmerized by the sway of her hips.

"Never," I said. And I meant it. I didn't think anyone had ever cooked for me.

"You've had to take care of yourself all these years," she said. "All these centuries. You deserve to be pampered for once."

I smiled. "Then I'll let you cook for me. Starting tomorrow."

"Well, technically, it's already tomorrow. But I'm too tired now. I'll let you do it."

She slipped into the bathroom, and I went downstairs to prepare a board with meat, cheese, and vegetables for the both of us.

Frost was sleeping in front of the dying fire. I threw two logs into the fire to revive it, and Frost opened one eye to look at me, then closed it and went back to sleep. Our little adventure in the snowstorm had worn him out.

In the kitchen, I first checked on Fluffy. The bunny was sleeping in his box. He'd eaten the carrot and promptly eliminated it, which meant that the box was now smelly and had to be cleaned. I scooped him up and looked around for a good place to relocate him. If I simply left him on the table, he would probably start hopping around, getting himself lost once more, this time under my furniture. Aura expected to see Fluffy when she came down, so I couldn't lose the damn creature. For lack of a better idea, I placed him in the breast pocket of my shirt.

I cleaned the box first, throwing Fluffy's mess outside, but then I saw he'd made himself comfortable in my pocket and gone to sleep, and I felt like I couldn't disturb him. Plus, Aura would appreciate that I was taking care of her pet. I heard her come down the stairs, so I started cutting the meat and cheese for our midnight snack.

She appeared in the doorway with Frost by her side. Great. So, he got up for her, but wouldn't get up for me.

"Sit down," I said.

"Thank you."

"Wine?"

"This late at night?" She laughed. "Wine not?"

"Sorry?" I was confused.

"It was a joke." She laughed harder. "Yes, wine sounds good. Thank you."

I poured her a glass, then went back to assembling the meat and cheese board.

"Where's Fluffy?"

"Right here."

I leaned in, and when she saw him in my breast pocket, she squealed.

"He is so cute! Look at him sleeping in there!"

But she couldn't help herself, so she scooped him out. The baby bunny woke up, and she squeezed him to her chest. I was glad to see he wasn't scared. He seemed to like being held. Frost went over to Aura and sniffed at her hands.

"Look, Frost. You have a new friend. His name is Fluffy."

Frost sniffed the bunny, and for a second, I froze, thinking the dog was going to open his massive jaws and swallow the tiny thing. He let out a whine instead, then shook his head and lay down at Aura's feet. I didn't know if that meant he accepted Fluffy as a pet, but for sure, it was a good sign. I'd have to keep an eye on them, though. Frost knew bunnies were generally food, not friends.

I finished arranging the board and placed it on the table. Aura and I ate with our hands and drank wine, and it turned out to be the best midnight snack I'd ever had.

"Starting tomorrow, I want to make an inventory of what's in the kitchen, the pantry, and the..."

"Cellar?"

"Yes!"

"Why?"

"So I can see what I can cook. I have a few dishes my mother used to make. I miss them so much. I hope you'll like them because I'll be making them this week."

"I will love everything you cook."

She laughed. "Don't be so quick to say that. Anyway, now that I can see..." She pointed at her eyes. "I can properly make this place my home."

My gaze dropped in shame. "I'm sorry I made you wear that mask."

She sighed, then reached to cover my hand with hers. "It wasn't so bad."

"You're still mad at me, and you have a right to be. I'll make it up to you, I promise."

"You're right, I'm still a little upset. I don't like that you lied to me, Krampus."

"I'm sorry."

"It's okay. I understand why you did it. But you must promise me you'll never do it again."

"I promise, of course."

"Okay. This will only work if we trust each other. And think about it... We're all alone here, in the mountains. We have Frost, Snowdrop, and now Fluffy. And we have each other. We're the only family we have, Krampus. This marriage has to be built on trust."

"I know." I looked into her beautiful golden eyes. I might've been centuries old, but my Aura was wiser than me. "I will never disappoint you again. You have my word. Even if it doesn't mean much..."

"Your word is all I need."

She placed Fluffy on the table and moved from her chair into my lap. I held her close to my chest, and we stayed like that for a few minutes, just listening to each other's heartbeat. Then Fluffy decided to inspect the meat and cheese board. He found the cherry tomatoes and placed his fluffy butt right in the middle of them. Diligently, he started munching on the tomatoes, one at a time.

Aura laughed. My first instinct was to shoo him away, but seeing her happy made me happy, so I let Fluffy eat the tomatoes. Never mind I'd painstakingly grew them in the greenhouse and now he was chewing on them like they'd been meant for him all along.

"This is nice," she said, picking up a piece of cheese and feeding it to me. "It's a slow, relaxed life, and I'm all for it. Back in town, I was always stressed because I was on my own, and there was so much to do. But here... it feels like time has slowed down, and we can enjoy every second without feeling guilty that we should be doing more. At least that's how I feel... I don't know about you."

"All I want is you, Aura. Life is perfect as long as I can have you."

I felt like that was the right answer. I wasn't sure what she was talking about, because my life had always been this way. Yes, it was slow and relaxed. I hadn't thought for a second that humans might live differently. I was glad I could offer my wife the comfort and peace of mind she deserved.

"You have me," she said. "And I have you."

She pressed her lips to mine. She tasted like red wine.

AURA

For once, I woke up before my husband. After what we'd done the night before, I'd slept like a baby and now felt refreshed and like I could take on the world.

One look outside the window told me that would have to wait. I doubted I could even open the door. Snow covered the landscape for as far as the eye could see. There was only white, the blue of the sky, and the dark forest in the distance.

I got dressed quietly, not wanting to wake Krampus, then made my way downstairs, where I was greeted by a very happy Frost. He followed me into the kitchen, where I started opening all the cupboards to see where everything was and inspected the fridge and the pantry.

"I'm not sure about your food," I told Frost. I looked for dog kibble in the pantry but couldn't find any. To be fair, I hadn't seen Krampus feed Frost that way. "How about some water?" That I could offer him.

As Frost lapped up the water, I found Fluffy in his box and fed him some fresh veggies. I'd never had a pet before, so this was all new to me. Well, I'd never had a husband before either... I didn't know what to feed his dog, but I knew what to feed him, so I started making breakfast.

Eggs, bacon, some sausages that I found in the fridge... It all went in a pan if it didn't go in Frost's eager mouth. A snack wouldn't hurt until Krampus could feed him and teach me how to make his food. I made batter for pancakes and sliced some fruit, and before I knew it, I had a rich breakfast waiting on the table. I covered everything the best I could, so it wouldn't get cold, then started cleaning up the mess I'd made. It would take me a while to get used to this kitchen.

I heard Krampus descend the stairs and smiled to myself. I couldn't wait to see the look on his face. His footsteps were heavy, which meant that I could always tell where he was in the house. He was in the living room now, throwing more logs into the fire, then he made his way to the kitchen, where he stopped in the doorway.

"Good morning," I called.

He just stood there, mouth agape.

"You did all this?" he said.

I huffed. "Of course I did all this. Did you think I don't know how to cook?"

"No, I... No, of course not. I just thought I would always do it for you."

"You can still cook for me," I said in a seductive voice. "From time to time."

Before we sat down to eat, Krampus took out a whole cooked chicken from the fridge and gave it to Frost. I didn't mention the snacks, but Frost and I exchanged a look.

"This is delicious," Krampus said as he dug in.

"I'll make my mother's special stew later today," I said.

"So, you're taking over the kitchen..."

I laughed. "I'm taking over the house."

He leaned down to plant a kiss on the top of my head.

"Now that I can see, I want you to show me everything," I said.

"I will give you a proper tour."

After breakfast, the priority was for Krampus to clean up a path between the cabin and the house while I did the dishes. Frost went to help him, and once I was done in the kitchen, I made myself a cup of tea and went to sit by the window to watch them. I saw a crow descend onto Frost, and I thought at first the bird was attacking him, but then realized they were playing. This must've been Frost's crow friend. He needed a name.

Krampus went to feed Snowdrop. I couldn't wait for him to be back, but I understood there were certain routines that needed to be done at certain times. I was going to get used to it soon enough. For the past year, I'd only had to take care of myself, and I wasn't proud to admit that my life had become a little chaotic because of it.

Krampus made his way back inside, but Frost stayed outside with his crow friend.

"King," I said.

"What?"

"We should name the crow King. I think it suits him."

Krampus laughed and shook his head. "I don't know where you get these names, but I admit that crow behaves like royalty sometimes. Bird royalty. King it is."

I finished my tea, then we started with the ground floor, which also came with the first surprise – Krampus had a workshop! It was behind a door that was always closed. I'd thought it was just another room, but when he held the door open for me, I saw walls covered in shelves that were chock full of craft materials. Various kinds of leather, whole pelts, fabrics in an array of colors, and tools that I didn't even know the name or the use of. In a box, he had yarn. I went straight to it and made an inventory of the colors. I took the spools out of the box and lined them up on the table.

Krampus came to sit next to me. "Everything that's mine is yours," he said. "I know you love knitting."

"I do. My mother taught me, and she learned from her mother. It's something my family has done for generations. Knitting saved me after my parents' passing, and not just financially. As my hands do all the work, my mind can escape."

"I feel the same when I'm in my workshop. It doesn't matter what I make. What matters is if I keep my hands busy, my mind is at ease."

I looked at him and felt my heart swell in my chest. We had so much in common.

"I brought my knitting needles with me," I said. "But all the yarn I had was destroyed in the fire."

He pushed the box toward me. "It's all yours. And you can use this space."

"Really? You don't mind? But it's your work-shop!"

He cupped my face with his big hands. "Aura, all that is mine is yours. You can come in here whenever you please."

"Okay. Thank you."

I couldn't stop touching the yarn spools. They gave me such a comforting feeling.

"You don't have my favorite color, though,"

His brows furrowed. "What's your favorite color?"

"Burgundy. You don't have it."

He chuckled and scratched the back of his neck. "Well..."

"You don't have yellow either. Or orange. Not a big fan of bright colors, I see."

"But there are three different shades of blue." He picked the yarn spools and showed them to me.

"Can we go buy burgundy? And the other colors we're missing?"

It was a small thing, so subtle, but his jaw tensed. His smile faded, and he proceeded to rearrange the yarn spools, as if they went in a certain order back in the box, and that was the only order that was acceptable.

"We also need more Christmas decorations. I brought some lights with me because I'd just bought them at the market before, you know, my house burned down..."

"So, you want to go into town..."

"Yes! We need to do some shopping! It will be fun."

He shook his head. "I don't know, Aura."

"Hey." I got up and positioned myself between his knees. "It will be different this time. In fact, from now on, it will always be different. Because we'll go shopping together, and the townspeople will see that you're not scary at all. I don't know everyone in town, but I know a few people. I will tell them how happy I am with you, and then they'll feel sorry for how they treated you."

"I don't want them to feel sorry..."

"They'll apologize!"

"I don't want them to apologize..." He sighed deeply. "I just don't want them to stare at me like I'm the most terrifying thing there is."

"Never again." I took his face between my hands and forced him to look into my eyes. "Listen to me, Krampus. Never again."

He smiled. "I believe you."

"Good! Because we need Christmas decorations, and I need my burgundy yarn."

He pulled me in, and our lips met in a fiery kiss. I wondered if this was his way of changing the subject. I could tell that even with my promise, he didn't feel comfortable going into town. I hated that I was putting him in an uncomfortable position, but at the same time, I felt like this needed to happen. I was certain that the moment he showed up with me by his side, the townspeople's opinion of him would change. It wasn't fair that it would be thanks to me, because truly, it should've been because he had such a big, kind heart, but if I could help, then I had every intention of doing it.

The town was my home. Well, my previous home. I didn't want to abandon it completely, and I wanted Krampus to enjoy it, too. I wanted us to enjoy it together. Since it so happened that the Temple had found me a match not far from where I was born, I wanted to visit it as often as I could.

I wanted to visit Mina and Joseph, too. But maybe it was too soon to suggest it to Krampus.

Krampus

The entire day, I couldn't stop thinking about what Aura had said about going into town. She wanted to buy yarn and Christmas decorations, but I knew that wasn't the only reason. My guess was that she missed it. This was only our third day together, isolated at the cabin, and I knew she was used to seeing people every day. She was used to living in a community.

She spent most of the day in the workshop, while I worked around the cabin. The snow needed to be shoveled often, and I took Snowdrop out for a walk. He loved the snow, just like Frost. Aura had Fluffy with her in the workshop. The two of them were inseparable, and I was of the opinion that she was feeding him too often. At this rate, he was going to be big in a few weeks, big enough for Frost to think Fluffy could provide dinner for three.

"What do you think?" I asked Snowdrop as I patted his neck. "Are you up for a trip into town?" I turned my head toward the sky. "It's letting up. It might not snow at all tomorrow." Snowdrop snorted, and I sighed. "I know, I know... But Aura wants to go. I can't say no to her."

Not that I didn't want to go shopping. I loved shopping. Too bad it had always been somewhat of an unpleasant experience. Aura thought that if the townspeople saw me with her, they would accept me, but I was afraid the effect would be the opposite.

What if seeing her with me made them hate me more? She was so beautiful and delicate. She was like a spring flower, and I was... well... I was me. What if seeing a monster like me with one of their own made them despise me more? I was certain there were young men in town who'd looked at Aura in the past and wanted her for themselves.

I spent the rest of the day making up scenarios in my head. I could see myself entering the grocery store in town with Aura on my arm, and the people snarling at us. I could see women pulling Aura aside and whispering to her that she should break up with me for her own good. With such images swirling around in my head, it was hard to focus. What brought me back to the present was Aura's delicious stew we had for lunch. It was so good that I asked her if we could have the same thing for dinner. She laughed and promised to make more.

Night came, and we found ourselves in bed, embraced, our limbs tangled as I entered her slowly. She moaned against my neck and clung to me, driving me deeper and deeper inside her. Her body was flexible and submissive, her skin sensitive to every touch, every kiss. She opened up for me, and even though we were still at the beginning, just learning each other's bodies, I felt like her pussy received me better and deeper. Soon enough, I'd be able to bury myself inside her completely, but for now, I had to be careful not to hurt her.

"Stop teasing," she begged.

"I'm not..."

"You are. Move a little faster, please."

"I don't want to break you."

"You could never break me," she whispered, looking into my eyes.

She reached up and wrapped her fingers around my horns. A growl escaped my throat, and I thrust into her faster and harder, watching her face for any sign that she might be in pain. But all I could see was pleasure. I was pushing her closer and closer to the edge.

Having my cock inside her pussy was bliss. I never wanted to let go of her, never wanted to not be physically and emotionally attached to her. I increased the pace, and she started moaning loudly, until her moans turned to screams, and then she buried her face in my neck and bit me as she came.

Her passion was so raw, and even though she didn't bite me too hard, that small hint of pain turned me on and made me come inside her much too soon. I filled her to the brim, and then I filled her some more, until my seed started seeping out of her and onto the sheets.

At this rate, we were going to have to change the sheets twice a day.

As I held her close, I whispered in her ear, "We can go shopping tomorrow."

She looked up at me. "Really?"

"Yes. We can go as often as you want. It's your town, and I know you miss it."

Her gaze softened. "I kind of miss it, yes. But I love it here."

"I know. I just want you to be happy, so we'll do whatever you want, whenever you want."

She wrapped her arms around my neck and kissed me. My cock was still inside her, as hard as ever. It didn't matter how many times I came. It seemed like these days, I was constantly hard, constantly craving her. I started thrusting again, and all the cum I'd filled her with provided enough lubrication that it allowed me to push my cock inside her completely.

"Oh," she gasped. "That feels amazing. Don't stop."

I never intended to stop.

AURA

The sky was clear. It hadn't snowed at all during the night, so we left early in the morning, right after breakfast. Snowdrop pulled the sleigh easily but walked slowly, careful on the winding road that hadn't been cleared because no one came up here. When the snow was too much, Krampus would get the shovel and clear the path for Snowdrop. Frost was impatient, running ahead, then turning back and barking, as if to chastise us for being so slow.

I didn't feel comfortable leaving Fluffy alone, but my husband had convinced me. Fluffy was too small, and carrying him around in his box would've been difficult. I made Krampus promise he would build him a proper house and something to carry him in, too.

The trip was long, made even longer by the road conditions, but we weren't in a hurry. When we finally saw the town in the distance, I pulled at my husband's sleeve.

"Let's go to the market," I said. "We will find everything we need there."

He stared at me with wide eyes. "I never go to the market."

"Where do you shop, then?"

"The grocery store at the edge of town. And I sometimes go to the bookstore, but I've been avoiding it lately because, you know, it's close to the center."

"But the best things are at the market!"

"That's right in the center of the town."

I pouted. Okay, what he was saying made sense. But now he was with me, and I didn't care what the townspeople thought about Krampus. They were going to change their mind today.

"I want to go to the market," I said. "Trust me, we'll get better deals."

Krampus sighed but pulled at the reins, and Snowdrop took the road that led to the town center. Seeing where we were headed, Frost became more mindful of his frolicking. He stuck close to the sleigh and didn't bark once when we entered the town proper.

I understood why people would be afraid of Frost. He was huge. The day before, when I came out of the workshop for a glass of water, he rushed at me, eager to play, and knocked me down without even trying. One minute, I was on my way to the kitchen, the next, I was on my back, with Frost on top of me, looking slightly confused. When he jumped on Krampus like that, Krampus didn't fall. Well, it was different with me. Poor thing, he'd seemed very apologetic.

Close to the market, we found a spot where we could leave Snowdrop and the sleigh. Krampus told Frost to wait, and Frost listened to him without complaint. Then Krampus took my hand, and we entered the market like the newlywed couple that we were.

As we made our way between the stalls, the chatter died down and all eyes were on us. People weren't even discreet. I spotted a few of my neighbors and waved at them. To my relief, they waved back, even if it was clear they were shocked.

"I don't like this," Krampus leaned in to whisper to me.

"Just act normal. Pretend like you don't notice that they're staring at us. Soon enough, they'll get bored and go back to their business."

Because that was what the market was about – business. Well, gossip too. I wasn't going to tell Krampus that.

I found my favorite yarn seller and stopped in front of her stall.

"Hi, Katrina! How have you been?"

"Aura! What a surprise! I heard what happened. I'm so sorry."

I shrugged. "Bad luck, I guess."

"Yes, but it was your house. Your parents' house! I can't even imagine."

"It was terrible, but it was all for the best in the end." I looked up at Krampus. He was standing next to me, and he was so awkward that I just wanted to give him a hug. I wrapped my arm around his biceps instead and pulled him closer. "This is my husband, Krampus."

Katrina looked up at him, her eyes as wide as saucers. For a second, she didn't know what to say, then she remembered her manners, smiled and waved.

"Hello, sir. Pleased to meet you."

Shocked, Krampus returned the pleasantry, then said, "You have quality yarn here. These colors are beautiful."

"Thank you. Feel free to choose what you like."

Krampus and I chose a few spools, and Katrina packed them up for us. As he paid, I couldn't help but feel proud of him. He was much more relaxed and even made small talk. We thanked Katrina, then moved on to check out the stalls that sold Christmas decorations. Soon enough, more and more people were willing to make small talk with Krampus, and he participated with enthusiasm. He even talked about the weather with an old man who was selling minia-ture Christmas trees made from wood and paper.

"No one has ever talked about the weather with me," Krampus told me later, when we were getting mulled wine.

I laughed. "You know so much about snowstorms that I'm sure a lot more people will come to you with questions." It was true. Krampus had taught the man what signs to look for that announced an impending storm. "Oh, let's get gingerbread cookies!"

He paid for the mulled wine and my snacks, and we spent another hour looking at what people had to sell. We ran into a few of my old clients, and they asked me if I was still knitting.

"Yes! I can't imagine not knitting."

"Will you have anything for sale soon?"

I bit the inside of my lip and looked up at Krampus. At first, he didn't know what I wanted from him. I wasn't sure what I wanted. Permission? I hadn't thought about selling my knitted items at the market now that I was married and living pretty far from town.

"Aura is preparing a new collection," Krampus said, taking me by surprise.

"Yes. When it's ready, I'll reclaim my old stall at the market, for sure," I said. Speaking of which, I'd noticed that the stall I usually rented was unoccupied.

The lady who'd asked smiled brightly and went on her way.

"Won't you mind bringing me into town every month to sell my stuff?" I asked Krampus.

We were making our way to the exit.

"Not at all. I like the market. You were right! This is much better than the store I used to go to. Maybe

I can sell some of the things I make. What do you think?"

I laughed. "I think it's a brilliant idea, don't get me wrong, but you'd have to take size into consideration."

"You're right. But that's good news. Smaller clothes, decorations, and pieces of furniture means less material used."

"And that's how a businessperson thinks!"

"Or a business monster," he chuckled.

Right before we exited the market, a stall caught my eye.

"Wait. I need to get one more thing," I said.

Krampus followed me. When we stopped in front of the stall, I could sense his surprise. Everything that was on display was for... babies. A ridiculous array of toys, and the smallest, most adorable clothes. I touched some of the clothes, but I wasn't sure whether I should pick pink or blue.

"Aura?" he asked me reluctantly.

I picked a stuffed teddy bear and a brightly colored set of wood blocks. "What do you think? Which one is better for a super small baby? Or we can buy both."

"But... why?"

I laughed. "Oh, don't get ahead of yourself. I just thought we could visit my friend, Mina, since we're in town, anyway. Her baby is due any time now, and I really want to see her and make sure she's doing okay."

"Visit your friend?"

"Why not?"

He stammered. "Be-because I've never visited someone before. I mean, I've never been to a human's house before."

I turned to the seller and told him I would buy the bear and the block set. Krampus hurried to pay, though he didn't look or sound very convinced about the visit.

"It will be great, you'll see," I assured him.

"I don't know, Aura. I can take you there and wait for you with Snowdrop and Frost."

"Nonsense! Mina and Joseph will love meeting you. And you'll love meeting them. They're my best friends ever. I don't know what I would've done without Mina after... you know... I lost my house."

He nodded. "Okay. I'll give it a try. For you. I'll be on my best behavior."

I laughed and nudged him teasingly. "You're always on your best behavior, my dear husband."

KRAMPUS

The fact that I couldn't say no to Aura was going to be the death of me. Well, not literally, now that I knew humans could be nice once they got to know me a little. But she was putting me in situations that required me to step way out of my comfort zone.

Following her directions, I drove us to her friend's house.

"Mina is not expecting us, is she?" I asked.

"No, but she'll love the surprise. It will be great, you'll see."

It was hard for me to be as optimistic as she was. I remained silent and found the house, then got off and helped Aura down. This time, Frost would not wait outside. He walked to the front door with us, and I tried to shoo him a few times, but Aura pulled at my sleeve, scolding me.

"Let him come with us. Mina and Joseph love animals."

She knocked on the door, and it was all I could do to not turn on my heel and bolt. I stood behind her, painfully aware of my height. I was taller than the door! And wider too. To get into the house, I would have to fold myself somehow, or turn sideways and shuffle in. It was going to be an embarrassment, and I would make a decent impression on exactly no one.

A dark-haired woman with a round belly opened the door. At the sight of my wife, she beamed, but then she looked past Aura's diminutive stature and saw me. Next to me, she saw Frost, who was wagging his tail like mad. Her smile dropped.

"Joseph," she called out. "We have guests!"

Aura ignored the way her friend's face had just blanched and jumped into her arms.

"Mina! You're not upset I dropped by unannounced, are you? I didn't know for sure I could come, and I wouldn't have been able to let you know in advance, anyway. These past few days have been intense! I missed you so much!"

"I missed you too," Mina said, embracing Aura. She didn't look away from me, though.

A man with blond hair and blue eyes appeared behind her. He did a double take, and I got the impression he wanted to run back inside and grab something, maybe a weapon, but then he steeled himself when he saw Aura, and even forced a smile to his thin lips.

Aura reached for my hand and pulled me forward.

"This is my husband, Krampus. I really wanted you to meet him."

The humans and I greeted each other in a reserved, polite manner.

"Come in," Joseph said. "Mina will make..." He exchanged a glance with his wife. "Tea?"

"Yes. I'll put the kettle on," Mina said.

"I'll help," Aura offered.

And now for the part that I was dreading. Aura slipped inside, and after her, Frost, who got plenty of pets from both Mina and Joseph. They were impressed by his size, but not put off. At this point, I was convinced it was easier to exist in the world as an oversized dog than an oversized... Krampus.

Sideways, bend down, shuffle... Shuffle some more, hit head on the door header, bend some more, shuffle-shuffle... Lose. Dignity.

Finally, I was inside their miniscule entry hall. From there, one big step of mine was enough to get me into the living room, where the only place I could sit was the couch, which I occupied entirely with my frame. Aura and Mina disappeared into the kitchen, while Joseph busied himself with the fireplace. There was no need for more wood to be thrown in, but he did it anyway, just to have a reason to turn away from me without making it too obvious.

I took this time to study my surroundings. The house was tiny compared to my cabin. I guessed it worked for two people, but I wasn't sure there was enough space to raise children, especially if they wanted more than one.

"Thank you for your generous donation," Joseph said, standing up to face me. "When winter is over, I will use part of the credits to expand the house a little. Mina and I wanted to add another room for quite a while. And the rest we will save for when our son or daughter comes of school-age. Hopefully, we can send him or her to a private school."

I looked at him like he was speaking in tongues. I blinked once, twice, trying to wrap my head around what he was saying. Donation? What donation?

"Mina and I didn't want to let Aura send her blood to the Temple. After her house burned down, she moved in with us, and we would've gladly let her live with us forever. She and Mina have been best friends since they were children." He was still standing with his back to the fireplace, in a rather awkward stance, with his hands in his pockets. "But now I'm glad she didn't listen to us, because she seems... happy."

The two women emerged from the kitchen. On two trays, they brought tiny porcelain cups – tiny for me, at least – cookies and sugar cubes. Aura sat down on the armrest of the couch, half on top of me. I wasn't sure if I was allowed to touch her or not. What would her friends think if I put my hand around her waist?

Joseph brought a chair for Mina and one for himself. I felt bad that I was occupying so much space and forcing them to adapt.

"Oh, let's show them what we got for the baby," Aura said excitedly.

I pulled out the two presents. They were small enough to fit into my coat pockets. Aura had asked the man we'd bought them from to wrap them up, and it wasn't immediately obvious what they were.

"It's not much," she said as she passed the gifts to Mina. "I know nothing about babies."

"Thank you so much," Mina said. She unwrapped the teddy bear and showed it to her husband. "You shouldn't have." She looked at me. "Especially after what you've already done for us."

"Oh, it was nothing," Aura said. "Don't even mention it. You helped me so much after my parents passed, and then after the house... Well, better not talk about it anymore. You needed the credits more than I did."

The credits! I'd paid the Temple for the service of providing me with a perfect match, and the priest had asked Aura what she wanted to do with the credits. It was weird that Joseph called it a donation. If it was a donation, then Aura had made it, not me.

"I just want to say that my wife wanted you to have the money. I just did my part and paid the Temple," I said.

"Thank you, nonetheless," Joseph said.

I nodded, and then Mina poured tea for all of us. As I did my best to use the tiny cup without breaking it, Aura dominated the conversation. She told them about our home, about Snowdrop and Frost – who was currently snoozing at our feet – and even about Fluffy and King. For a second, I was worried she was going to tell them about how I'd made her cover her eyes, but she didn't. She only talked about the good things and didn't even mention the snowstorm and how she'd gotten lost and almost died. She told them about the greenhouse, the workshop, and explained that we came into town to buy yarn and Christmas decorations.

"So, you'll come into town more often?" Mina asked.

"If you don't mind having guests once or twice a month, definitely," Aura said.

"We can come every week, if you want," I told Aura.

She turned to me. "Really?"

"When the weather is good."

"I'd love that!" She turned to Mina and Joseph. "Don't worry, we won't bother you that often. I just love going to the market. And I'll start knitting again! My old clients are still interested."

Mina stood up then and came to hug Aura. "I'm so glad everything has worked out for you. Just so you know, Joseph and I have been thinking about you a lot."

"You shouldn't have worried," Aura said. "I told you not to worry."

"You know how she is," Joseph said about Mina. "Tell her to not do something, and she goes and does exactly that."

We laughed, and I noticed how relaxed I felt. I even ate a cookie.

We spent another hour with Mina and Joseph. While the women talked about baby things, Joseph and I talked about how he could better add a new room to the house. I offered to come help him, and to my utter surprise, he accepted. When Aura said it was time to go and I realized the visit was over, I felt a bit sad. We said our goodbyes, and when I helped her into the sleigh, she whispered in my ear,

"You've made a friend. Don't worry, we'll visit more often."

"A friend?"

"Yes. Joseph. He likes you."

I got into the sleigh with her. Mina and Joseph waved at us, and we waved back.

"Nah, he doesn't like me," I said. But I was smiling to myself. "He was just being polite."

"No, he meant it when he said he could use your help this spring. By then, the baby will be here, and I'll help Mina. They need us. Which is a good thing, because I'll need Mina too."

"What for?"

Snowdrop was happy to be moving again. Frost ran ahead of the sleigh.

"For when I'll be in her position," Aura said, cuddling to my side. "Big, and round, and heavy, and terrified that I'm not ready to be a mother." She chuckled.

I was stunned. Was she talking about having babies? So soon? Because I was in.

"She's glowing, though," she continued. "Do you think I'll glow when I get pregnant?"

I looked at her like she was the most beautiful woman in the world. Because she was.

"You're glowing already, my wife. And I believe you'll glow even more."

She giggled and hid her face in my arm.

AURA

What we knew about Christmas came from ancient books that had survived the Shift. There weren't a lot of them, and most had missing pages and even entire chapters that had been lost and impossible to reproduce. There was a lot we didn't know about this holiday, like why it was called Christmas, and why the people who lived on Alia Terra before the Shift chose to celebrate it in winter. We did know that gifts were exchanged on the first day of Christmas, and that we were supposed to decorate our houses and our yards prior to it. Some people took an entire tree inside and decorated it, but I personally never understood this tradition. I was glad to see that Krampus didn't favor it, either.

The second I got the yarn that I wanted, I set about to work on the Christmas presents I was going to give my husband, Frost, and Snowdrop. Fluffy was going to get something, too. I spent every minute I had knitting. It was a good thing I loved it and my fingers were used to the effort, otherwise I might not have finished in time.

Christmas Day came much too soon. Because I'd been so busy knitting, Krampus took care of Christmas dinner. I was eternally grateful to him. I cooked too, but I had to admit that he was simply better at it than I was. It had snowed all day, and I hated it that we wouldn't be able to visit Mina and Joseph because of how bad the roads were, but it was cozy inside, and I had my husband. What more could I ask for? I had never been greedy, and I wasn't going to start now.

Before dinner, we gathered in front of the fireplace. Krampus and I sat in front of each other, ready to exchange gifts, and Frost was at our feet, his ears perked in anticipation. He wasn't sure what was happening, but he knew it was different from our daily routine. Fluffy was in my lap, munching on a biscuit. Snowdrop was in the barn, of course. I was going to bring him his gift later.

"I'll go first," I said. "I didn't have much time, so... I'm afraid Frost gets the best present."

I pulled out a sweater that I'd knitted for him. For some reason, I'd gotten this knitting pattern in my head, and I started making the sweater before I realized it would take me forever to make it in my husband's size. Lucky Frost.

Krampus laughed out loud. I frowned, and he apologized, saying, "It's lovely. But Frost has never worn a sweater. Let's see if he'll let us put it on him."

The dog sniffed his present thoroughly before allowing us to dress him up. We struggled to make him understand he needed to put his front legs through the two holes, and when the sweater was finally on, I was tired and sweaty. Krampus seemed to be just fine, but the whole process had been a workout for me.

"And this is for you," I told Krampus as I gave him his gift.

He tore into it quickly, grinning, and pulled out a scarf that was in the same colors as Frost's sweater. He hugged it to his chest and looked at me with what I could only call puppy eyes.

"Thank you so much," he said. "No one has ever knitted something for me before."

My eyes widened. "Better get used to it. I'm already thinking about what I'm going to knit for your birthday."

His smile fell. "I don't know when my birthday is, Aura."

I set Fluffy down and moved to press myself to my husband's chest. He wrapped his big arms around me.

"I know. That's why I think you should choose a day, and that will be your birthday. What's your favorite season?"

"Spring."

"Then you should choose a day in spring," I said.

He hesitated for a moment, considered it, then said, "I'll think about it."

I knew this was a difficult topic for him, so I let it go for the time being. Snowdrop's present was next, and I let Krampus unpack it. It was another scarf, smaller and less practical, because it wasn't like Snowdrop needed a real scarf, but I wanted him to have something that matched Krampus and Frost.

Krampus laughed again. "This is hilarious. I love it!"

"The three of you will look like brothers."

We laughed together, then it was Fluffy's turn. For him, I'd made a little pillow in the same colors. I'd noticed that he loved sleeping on my pillow when I took him upstairs, or on the couch pillows. Now that he had his own, maybe I wouldn't need to wash the other pillowcases as often.

"Are you ready for your gift, my wife?" Krampus asked me.

My heart started pounding in my chest. He pulled out a square box, and I had no idea what it could be. I opened it with trembling hands, and when I saw what was inside, I gasped.

The most beautiful choker I'd ever seen!

My mother had never owned jewelry. My parents didn't have credits to spend on such things, so I'd never owned or worn jewelry either.

"You made this?" I asked.

"Yes. Do you like it?"

"It's the most beautiful thing I've ever seen!"

No precious metals were involved, but the design was stunning. It was made of soft leather, and the medallion was made of resin. Inside it, I could see leaves and flowers. It was rather big. Krampus helped me put it on, and it covered the entire top part of my chest. It looked incredible! I was never going to take it off. Well, except when I slept and bathed.

I climbed on top of him and grabbed him by the horns. When I did that, he knew things were about to get serious. In the most pleasant and delicious way. I kissed him deeply, and he pulled me close until I could feel him grow hard. I ground my hips against him, and he let out a low groan. Things were getting heated, but then Frost decided to interrupt us with a bark. Krampus and I pulled away, laughing.

"He's right," I said. "It's time for dinner."

"Look at you speaking Frost fluently."

I punched him teasingly and stood up, smoothing down my skirt. "Come on. I'm starving."

"Right this way, my beautiful wife. I have prepared a feast for you."

I laughed and let him lead me to the table that he'd set up in the living room. Frost and Fluffy had to be fed first, of course. I didn't mind. I loved watching Krampus take care of all of us, one at a time. Finally, he sat down and poured wine into our glasses.

"Merry Christmas," he said.

"Merry Christmas." I took a sip, then wondered out loud. "Do you know why we say that?"

"No idea," he said. "But I do know that it's merry, indeed."

I laughed. "You know what? With you, every day of the year is merry."

KRAMPUS

This was the longest winter of all. Technically, it was spring, but it still snowed some days, and Aura and I preferred to cozy up in the cabin, in front of the fire, than be outside. Since Christmas, we'd visited Mina and Joseph a few times. Mina had had her baby, and Aura had asked me to let her stay with them for a few days, so she could help. I went to see her every day, even though Snowdrop had grown bored with going up and down the mountain. Mina and Joseph had a baby girl, and they named her Amalia.

Now that the baby was here, Joseph was restless. We'd decided to start working on his project in a week, so as I watched Aura knit and Frost snore with Fluffy on top of him, I looked outside and shook my head when I saw it was snowing again.

"What are you thinking about?" asked Aura.

"That I'm tired of winter."

She chuckled. "Me too. Well, what can we do? Stay inside, read, knit... think about baby names."

My ears perked. "Baby names?"

She shrugged, but I could tell she was acting nonchalantly on purpose. "Better start early."

I moved away from the window and came to sit next to her. The couch dipped under my weight, and Aura giggled when she inevitably rolled toward me.

"What are you saying?" I asked.

"I'm saying that... mmm... hm. What am I saying?"

"You're such a tease."

She laughed and set her knitting needles aside. She looked me in the eye. She was beaming.

"What I'm saying is that I am pregnant."

I held my breath for a moment, then exhaled. I was so tense I couldn't move. I didn't want her to get the wrong impression, but I genuinely didn't know how to react. I knew this day would come, but that didn't mean I was prepared for it.

"Are you sure?" I asked.

She rolled her eyes. "When I last visited Mina, I did a pregnancy test. Yes, I'm sure." She touched her stomach lightly.

"This is... This is..."

I had no words, so I pulled her in my arms and held her there.

"Krampus," she mumbled against my chest. "Can 't... breathe..."

"Oh, I'm sorry..." I let her go, and she took a few deep breaths before beaming at me again. "This is... incredible. A dream come true. A dream I hadn't dared to dream for a long, long time. For most of my life."

"I know."

She was happy, but I was somber. Because she didn't know what it meant to me.

"Aura, do you understand?" I touched her belly with reverence. "A tiny Krampus is growing inside you, and when he or she is here, I won't be the only one in the world anymore."

Her smile faded and her eyes turned gentle. She cupped my face with her hands.

"I understand," she said. "I am sure the baby will look just like you."

"It won't bother you?"

"Not at all. Our baby will be perfect."

I smiled. "I hope he or she has your eyes."

"I hope he or she has your hair."

She laughed, and I joined her. We spent the rest of the evening throwing around baby names and making plans for the future. A few months ago, I wouldn't have dared to think that I would ever experience such joy. Now here I was, my heart full of it, realizing for the first time that it was only going to get better and better.

It was all because of Aura. She'd changed my life and my entire world, and to show her how grateful I was, I was going to work hard to make myself worthy of her.

This was my purpose.

Arranged Monster Mates

Wed to the Ice Giant, by Layla Fae

Wed to the Minotaur, by Eden Ember

Wed to the Wolfman, by Cara Wylde

Wed to the Phoenix, by Eden Ember

Wed to the Dragon, by Cara Wylde

Wed to the Orc, by Layla Fae

Wed to the Lionman, by Cara Wylde

Wed to the Lich, by Layla Fae

Wed to the Bullman, by Eden Ember

Wed to Jack Frost, by Layla Fae

Wed to the Dark Elf, by Eden Ember

Wed to the Gargoyle, by Eden Ember

Wed to the Grendel, by Cara Wylde

Wed to the Basilisk, by Layla Fae

Monster Security Agency

Printed in Dunstable, United Kingdom